Bears of England

Bears of England

Mick Jackson

faber and faber

First published in 2009
by Faber and Faber Limited
Bloomsbury House, 74–77 Great Russell Street,
London WC1B 3DA

Typeset by Faber and Faber
Printed and bound in the UK by CPI Mackays, Chatham ME5 8TD

A CIP record for this book
is available from the British Library

ISBN 978–0–571–24240–5

2 4 6 8 10 9 7 5 3 1

Bears of England

1

Spirit Bears

In the days before electric light and oil lamps, the night imposed its own abysmal tyranny, and daylight's surrender was measured out in strict division. *Sunset* gave way to *Twilight*, just as *Evening* preceded *Candle-Time*. *Bedtime* was hope's last bastion. Beyond that, there was nothing but *Dead of Night*.

Dead of Night was like an entombment – a heavy stone slowly lowered onto every home. It eclipsed the past and obscured the future. Hope and reason crept away. And in their absence the world was altered. The night's actions were a mystery.

Filled to the brim with every sort of ignorance and superstition, no Englishman would dare venture out at Dead of Night, for fear of being swallowed up by it. Every door was locked and bolted, and remained so right through those awful hours, until deliverance finally arrived at first cock-crow. Prior to that, every

scratch and scrape, every rattle of leaf was thought to be the work of some demon, some twisted malevolence out among the trees. And in the villagers' imagination that evil found its most common incarnation in the form of Spirit Bears.

These night-time bears would come by in ones and twos, clawing at doors and windows, and on stormy nights run riot in great gangs and turn the whole place upside down. Then, just before dawn they would slip away, back down the secret paths to their own wild world.

Whenever a villager sensed the presence of a Spirit Bear it was traditional to blow on an old goat's horn, to warn the neighbours. But, as anyone who's had the misfortune to hear such a thing will testify, a goat's horn produces the most mournful sound imaginable, capable of inducing a mood of utter wretchedness in even the sunniest soul. What's worse, as each neighbour was alerted they would take up their own goat's horn and do their own bit of blowing. So that in no time at all the night would be awash with a goat's horn chorus and any prospect of sleep would be well and truly dashed.

'*Bears abroad*,' the horns insisted. '*Bears abroad*.'

At that time, most of England was bedevilled, to some degree or other, by bear-spirits, but one village in particular had managed to drive itself to the very verge of distraction – a small hamlet of no more than twenty dwellings, which clung to the edge of one of the larger woods.

The inhabitants were of the opinion that they had long been under siege by an especially wicked gang of Spirit Bears and had done everything in their power to ward them off. They had tied old rags to the branches of trees along the wood's perimeter and cast quantities of salt, in a variety of significant shapes and patterns, across the woodland floor. But the bears persisted. Until, in the end, the villagers decided that the only way to resolve the

situation was to send one of their number out into the woods to try and inveigle their way among them and, if possible, to negotiate.

After much discussion and casting of votes it was unanimously decided that the villager best suited to such a task was Awd Tom, his candidacy based in no small part on the fact that he was old (as his name suggested), somewhat slow on the uptake, and without a wife or children, so that

if, heaven forbid, he should go off into the woods and not come back his absence might not be too keenly felt.

Tom was informed of the decision when he returned from a kindling-gathering expedition. He rather had a hunch that something was afoot. The entire village had lined the lane, and were cheering and applauding him, which, as far as he could remember, had not happened after any previous kindling-gathering trip.

When he heard the news he was momentarily flattered – proud, even – to be trusted with such a responsibility. But the daunting nature of his little mission soon began to make itself known to him, and continued to make itself known, in ever more vivid detail, for all the hours leading up to him being sent out into the dark.

Soon after sunset, two of the older women led him round to one of the barns and set about dressing him in such a manner that he might move among the bears without drawing too much attention. The bears were woodland creatures, the women reasoned, and would in all likelihood, be made up of such stuff to be found in such a place. So with lengths of twine they bound twigs and moss about him, then wove leaves and kindling in between, adorning Awd Tom so comprehensively with foliage, that by the time they were done and he took a walk up and down the barn, the weight and hindrance of all those bits of twig and branch quite transformed him. And this so unsettled the women that they made their excuses and headed home to take strong drink to calm their nerves.

The arrival of Twilight filled Awd Tom with even more anxiety than usual, and round about Candle-Time, Young Peter, a man who had high hopes of one day being the village's leader (and prime mover behind Tom's nomination earlier in the day), came by to offer a little encouragement.

'The way I see it,' he told the man in the suit of moss and twigs, 'to be able to move among the bears without being too conspicuous, you must do your utmost to *think* like a bear.'

He stopped, to see if his words had penetrated the bark and bracken. Two eyes blinked, deep amid the twigs.

'One might almost say . . .' Peter paused, to try and

find the right way of putting it, '. . . that you must *become* a bear,' he said.

Awd Tom remained quite silent, but his eyes darted to left and right, which Young Peter took as a sign of cognition. Then Peter wished him well and went off to barricade himself in his cottage, like everyone else.

None of the villagers witnessed Tom's final preparations. In fact, as time passed Awd Tom himself had an ever-weakening grasp of what went on in that old barn. For, as instructed, he did his utmost to assume a bear-like physicality and an ursine state of mind, which culminated in a series of ritualistic movements that so possessed him he slowly became aware how he left behind his Awd Tom-ness and began to inhabit a much wilder, more primitive place.

Through the shuffled steps of his own strange invocation and the gradual abandonment of his civilised mind he induced in himself something almost trance-like. Awd Tom's eyes became a bear's eyes. And the only thoughts in that tight briar of twig and bramble became those of a Spirit Bear.

By the time Dead of Night finally arrived every villager stood by their window, secretly sickened by their own part in the conspiracy, yet undeniably excited about what might come to pass. If they were hoping that Awd Tom might stage some grand departure, however, they were disappointed. All they caught was a fleeting glimpse of a leafy shadow as it hurried past them and disappeared into the trees.

As the night wore on the villagers kept their stations. The moon was down. There were the usual eerie bustles and scuffles, normally attributed to the agitations of the Spirit Bears, but among them now were unfamiliar yelps and screeches, and at one point a sustained period of whinnying, which fairly made the villagers' blood run cold.

The winter nights were always long but this was by far the longest. It seemed to last an eternity. After that initial flurry there was nothing but silence. The village had never known a stillness of such intensity and it terrified them almost as much as all the comings and goings of the Spirit Bears, until at last the first cock's crow broke the spell, the doors were thrown open and everyone raced out, to see if they could find any trace of dear Awd Tom.

A low mist covered the ground and the villagers stepped nervously into it. Their task wasn't helped by the fact that Tom's suit of leaf and twig created such a convincing camouflage. It was one of the children who finally found him, a fair way into the woods, slumped against a fallen tree. His eyes were open – wide open – but utterly vacant, as if the mind behind them still operated, but on a quite different plane.

The villagers bore him home, still decked out in all his foliage. Then the same women who'd so meticulously arranged the leaves and twigs around him now began to carefully pick those same leaves and twigs apart. It was several hours before Awd Tom was able to string a sentence together – long hours in which the women did their best to revive him by rubbing boiled hyssop into his shoulders and mopping his brow with tansy and valerian.

Before he had uttered a single word, the entire village gathered in the barn to see what sort of shape the old man had been reduced to and hoping for news regarding the bears. And after a while they managed to establish from his various grunts and nods in response to their many questions that he had indeed made contact with them, had moved among them and, most significantly, had struck some sort of deal.

'You mean, the bears are willing to settle?' said one of the villagers.

Awd Tom nodded.

'And they're willing to leave us in peace?' said another.

Tom nodded again.

This provoked a great deal of hugging and cheering, and quite a few tears of sheer, blessed relief. In the silence that followed, someone dared to ask, 'And do they want for anything in return?'

Awd Tom nodded his tired old head again, and lifted a finger – a finger still covered with the forest's own filth and dirt. His outstretched arm swung around the assembled company until it pointed squarely at Young Peter.

According to Tom's instructions, when he was finally able to articulate them (and which were, after all, nothing but the instructions passed on to him by the Spirit Bears), Young Peter was bound and left out in the woods in a rough sort of cage for three nights running, so that the Bears could get a closer look at him. Apparently, they

were intrigued by the incredible self-confidence in one of such tender years.

The first night was probably the worst for poor Peter. By the end of it his hair had turned quite white. But by the third night he had calmed down a fair bit, which is to say that he had stopped screaming and shouting and banging his head against the bars of his cage. And from that point forward Peter – or Quiet Peter as he came to be known – was much less prone to scheming and speechifying, and more likely to sit alone in a corner, fussing with an old scrap of leather or a piece of wood.

It is quite remarkable how much an individual's status can shift in such a short period. While Quiet Peter withdrew to the shadows, Tom came to the fore, assuming the role of something like a local shaman, which is quite a step up from kindling-gatherer. He lived a leisurely life, consulted on any matter which required a little wisdom, as befitted a man of his age. But once a year he would have the women dress him up in his suit of twigs and at Dead of Night go out into the woods, which only added to his reputation and, by all accounts, seemed to do him the world of good.

It is harder to say what became of the Spirit Bears. Depending on one's perspective, they either followed those secret paths and byways back to their own dark world or retreated into the deeper recesses of the villagers' imagination. But it would be a brave man who could say for certain which is the safer place for them.

2

Sin-Eating Bears

A bear must eat. It is a Law of Nature. A bear without food will quickly tend towards ill temper, and bad-tempered bears do nothing but make life difficult for everyone else. Indeed, it could be said that a bear's need for food is the very foundation of Anglo-bear relations. And that, in its way, such hunger brought about the only period in English history when the bear was accorded, first, respect, then, albeit briefly, something approaching reverence.

Early English Man had tried his hand at bear-consumption, with decidedly poor returns. The consumption, by necessity, had to be preceded by a little hunting, but just as every bear-hunt neared its natural conclusion the bear had a habit of turning the tables and making a meal of the very people who had been planning to dine on him.

Chastened, the Early English hunter-gatherer

retreated to his homestead to raise chickens and rabbits and other creatures which might more easily end up in the pot. And the bears were left to roam and generally go about their business, just as long as their business did not too greatly interfere with Early English Man.

This is possibly not the place to speculate whether the English are more prone to sinning than any other nation. Certainly, they are just as keen to remove any stain or blemish in this world before going on to the next. And it is here that the Common Bear, which had proved so unreliable when it came to being hunted, finally found a place for itself in Early English life.

A tradition had long existed whereby an individual of lowly means and meagre income, and in other words in want of a solid meal, would partake of bread and ale before a house in mourning, and in so doing, take on the sins of the departed prior to their Judgement Day.

It was a job no sane man would aspire to. In fact, it was the sort of job guaranteed to keep one at the very periphery of society. So it is no surprise that there came a point when such sin-eaters decided that they had had their fill. Perhaps the accumulated sin began to weigh too heavily on them. Perhaps they feared that when their own time came to meet their Maker no man or woman would be sufficiently hungry to take up their own lamentable load. But traditions change. Sometimes they evolve by increment. Sometimes that change happens overnight.

An old man died. At dawn, bread and ale was put out, according to convention. The widow-wife took up a seat beside her husband, who was laid out on his bed. The sun rose and slowly headed off across the firmament. The widow sat. The widow waited. In fact, she sat and waited right through the day. Outside, the bread grew stale; midges danced about the beer. But the eater failed to show.

At dusk the widow got to her feet and went and looked out of the window – was, in fact, about to fetch the bread and ale, when she saw a figure coming down the lane. She stood stock-still as the bear slowly advanced towards her. It was a middle-aged bear, slightly mangy, and as it ambled along it kept an eye out for any threat or sudden movement. At first, it went straight past the cottage. Then it stopped, backed up a little, and had another look.

In an ideal world, the widow later admitted, she would have had a human do the eating. But in the circumstances she was just grateful that the sins were being eaten up at all. As the bear dined she studied it, for any signs of corruption. She was well aware of several sinful acts which would require absolution and had suspicions regarding another two or three. But the bear just ate and drank with apparent indifference. It scratched an ear on a couple of occasions, but the widow decided not to read too much into that.

When the bear finished with the bread it brushed its paws together, to clean the crumbs off. Then it looked up and saw the old woman, watching at the window. On her life, she said, the brute looked directly at her, its eyes penetrating her so absolutely that she felt it examine her very soul. It duly identified her as the wife

of the fellow whose sins it had just ingested. And as it continued to hold her in its gaze the bear gave her a single solemn nod. Just a little one, she said, but unmistakable, as if acknowledging some of the misery she'd had to endure. Then it swigged the last of the beer, wiped its mouth with the back of a paw and carried on its way.

Within a matter of months the role of sin-eater had passed to hungry bear from hungry peasant. Of course, the bears were quite oblivious. All they knew was bread and beer. They were vaguely aware of the recent increase in its availability. They may even have had a suspicion that such stuff was being left out for them. But they had no notion of the service they were meant to be providing in return.

But this didn't hinder the way people chose to perceive them, which, increasingly, took on a mystical bent. Stories began to circulate of hunters, deep in the woods, stumbling upon Bear Conferences – secret ceremonies where a bear stood at a makeshift pulpit and preached to vast bear-congregations. Others spoke, in hushed tones, about the existence of Bear Monasteries, high up in the mountains – the sort of peaks unreachable by anything but a bear – where they would sit, for days on end and privately ponder the universe. One or two (admittedly mostly idiots and degenerates) even claimed to have lost their way or suffered some dreadful injury and regained consciousness in a cave-hospital, where they were tended by bears.

This marked the beginning of what has come to be known as the era of the Holy Bear: a sainted creature who could heal a man simply by raising a paw in his direction. And there was no shortage of otherwise quite sensible people prepared to testify that they had personally felt the benefit of the 'healing paw'.

With hindsight, such an estimation was plainly unsustainable, and so it proved to be. Their fall from grace was swift and brutal. They were cast out from their role as healer and mystic just as quickly as they had been sworn in. The change in attitude can be traced back to a particular incident when a bear, having eaten free bread and drunk free beer one evening, retired to its cave in order to get some sleep. It slept long and hard, but slowly found its dreams invaded by something *foreign*: human thought . . . human memory.

Something sinister had wormed its way into its psyche. The bear twitched and turned, but could not wake. Then it saw blood. Heard a voice cry, 'Murder!' Felt human guilt rise up and flood its soul.

The bear woke to find itself charging through the forest. It clutched its head as if it brimmed with bees. And without knowing why, the bear headed back towards the village where it had taken bread and ale the previous day.

The family and friends attending the funeral were unaware of what was about to befall them. They had attended a short service where thanks had been given, then followed the body as it headed to its final resting-place. The first sign of trouble was a distant howl from up in the woods. Only a handful of mourners heard it, and did not pay it too much attention. Their thoughts were with the fellow whose coffin was about to go into the ground.

The next thing they knew was a tremendous roar as the bear climbed the wall fifty yards away. Then it was among them. It came clattering through the graveyard, knocking over several stones and markers on its way. It roared again as it neared the graveside, but by that point people were running and screaming in every direction and the service had rather fizzled out.

The bear didn't seem to notice. It landed on the wooden box and within a matter of seconds had ripped it open. It grabbed the occupant and dragged him out. Some of the mourners, having run a little distance, couldn't help but stop and turn, to see what happened next. They saw the bear's huge head drop towards the dead man. They imagined that, having had its appetite whetted by bread and beer, it had returned for a more substantial meal.

In fact, it was quite the contrary. In four great heaves
the bear brought up the contents of its stomach. And
almost immediately, even as it crouched there getting its
breath back, the bear felt its condition improve. The
visions ceased, the pain abated. Whatever sins it had
taken on the previous evening had been ejected – and

returned to their rightful owner.

The bear stepped off the coffin and looked around it, which provoked another round of screaming and running. But the bear just took a moment to compose itself, then turned and headed back towards the woods. It felt a little queasy, but no worse than you or I might feel, having overindulged the previous night.

In that minute the era of Bear Worship was terminated and Bear Fear and Hatred was restored. The halo had slipped; the healing paw was neutered. The bear had rejected its role of assuager of English guilt and obliged the country's inhabitants to take responsibility for their own actions. And for that it would never be forgiven.

3

Bears in Chains

There is no category of bear whose story makes for more depressing reading, and whose miserable existence heaps more shame on humanity than that which follows. Readers of a nervous disposition may be tempted to skip this chapter and that, of course, is their prerogative. But there are at least two good reasons why they should continue reading. First, by omitting one of the longer chapters such readers will be reducing an already short book to little more than a pamphlet – a withered runt of a thing. More significantly, when they turn out the light at close of day, being of a nervous disposition, their imagination will return inexorably to that missing chapter, and will slowly furnish it with all sorts of horrors and ursine-cruelty which their sick mind is uniquely capable of conjuring up, and much worse, probably, than anything included here.

So, let us begin by laying down the bare bones of bear-baiting. Quite frankly, it is difficult to know where to start. Whether to start with the metal halter, the post buried in the middle of the arena and the length of heavy chain between them, or the bear's entrance and the roars and cheers which greeted it. Certainly we must mention the crowd – the hundreds, sometimes thousands, of ordinary people, brought together in their shared love of bear-sport, but all of them high enough up and well enough out of the way that even if a bear were to break free, they would be in no mortal danger – in fact, would be perfectly placed to watch the fun.

And then there are the dogs. And here they come. More cheers, gradually giving way to apprehensive silence. Dogs slowly circling and stalking, but all the while watching the bear. Then the first dog lunges and has a nip, before quickly retreating. Then two or three dogs attack at the same moment, at two or three different parts of the bear. And the crowd is on its feet now. And we are back to cheering. And the entertainment is well under way.

The bear will sometimes
fling a dog across the bear-
pit, sometimes smash it
with a paw, but it is
not unheard of for a
bear to grab a
dog and bring
it close, with
the dog's
jaws
still

snapping, to try and squeeze the life right out of it. And by now the dogs will have gauged the length of the chain between post and halter – will know exactly how many yards' clearance is required for them to be safe. And there is no lack of dogs. As the bear does its best to tackle one dog, the next comes at it. One or two may limp away, broken and bleeding, but now the rest are in a frenzy – they cannot help themselves. And all this ripping and tearing continues until every last dog has been put out of action, or the bear itself lies dead.

A child's first visit to a bear-pit must have been a bewildering business. Aside from the savagery taking place before them, there was the bloodlust of the crowd to endure. But one assumes that, with each consequent visit to the bear-garden these concerns and anxieties would gradually diminish. The atmosphere and the spectacle would grow familiar. Until, there would come a day when they too would suddenly get to their feet, baying and gesticulating, along with everyone else.

As for the bears themselves, it is difficult now to establish whether they were direct descendants of the native English bear or had been imported from further afield. For our purposes, however, we should regard them as English. They were, after all, bred in English captivity and killed in England for the entertainment of Englishmen. And, once killed, their corpses went into England's soil, where English worms slowly worked their way through them, as an English breeze erased their memory. So even if, at the time, the bears didn't consider themselves English, they are most certainly a part of England now.

Each night, the dead bears were carted off to a secret location and their bloody bodies rolled into a pit. The whereabouts of these sites was not made public, so it says a good deal about the persistence of the myth of the 'healing paw', or simple morbid curiosity, that on occasion individuals tracked down the sites, scaled the necessary walls and fences and evaded the night watchman in order to have a closer look. But only one man is known to have got among the corpses. His name was Henry Jacks. Jacks had taken a length of rope, hoping to tie it off against something such as a tree or post, then let himself down on it, but in the event no such tree or post was to be found. But as he stood at the edge of the pit and saw three or four paws among the carnage he must have convinced himself that the sides of the grave were not so steep as to prevent him climbing in and out, with the help of a few hand- and footholds along the way.

He got in easily enough and for the last few feet allowed gravity to take him. Then he began stepping among the bears. It was never clear whether he wanted the paw for himself or had arranged to sell it on to a third party. Wherever it was destined, he was found to have a saw's blade in his pocket, wrapped up in a piece of linen and a handkerchief masking his nose. But such a precaution was far from sufficient. If he'd only asked around he'd have learnt that for every three or four bears that went into the pit, several shovelfuls of quicklime went in

29

with them. And only as he crawled among the corpses and pulled a paw up here and there, did he feel his hands and knees begin to itch, then burn. And by the time he properly appreciated that something was amiss it was already too late.

He clambered over to the side and tried to pick his way back up the steep bank of earth. Tried to find those holes he'd used on his way in. But his hands were now too blistered to be of any use to him. He looked down at them as they burned by the moonlight. They were all blackened and bloated. And in those last few moments, before the full fire of the lime engulfed him they looked to Henry Jacks like the paws of a bear.

Nobody visited the pit the next day and when, the day after, four men came by, around about gloaming, they rolled the bears in right on top of poor old Jacks and added a generous dusting of quicklime, without noticing him. It took a while for Jacks' wife to report him missing and an extra day or two before she suggested where he might be found, by which time the lime had done its worst and it was generally felt that too much effort would have had to be expended to extract what was left of him, so the decision was made to leave him where he was.

It is a salutary lesson, although perhaps it's best to let the reader decide the particulars of what that lesson might be. But the death of Henry Jacks is not our primary interest, so we too should leave him a-mouldering and turn our attention to a bear which beat off the dogs and escaped the burial pit – a bear whose actions had a tremendous bearing on the fate of all the rest. But in order to introduce this creature, we must first explain how a bear which consistently saw off its adversaries would gain a reputation and how an audience would begin to attend particular fixtures just to cheer it on, which is all the more peculiar when one considers that only a week or two earlier the same audience would have gone along in the hope of witnessing the same creature being ripped apart.

All the same, for those few bears which managed to

31

find their way into the public's affections, there was no knowing where the appreciation might end. Spectators would sew coloured scarves to their sleeves to denote their affiliation and carry placards with drawings depicting their favoured bear. Only thirty or forty bears ever achieved such a lofty status and it would seem that only one ever gained such popularity that its life was actually spared.

That bear was commonly known as 'Samson'. The similarities with the biblical character are twofold. The first and most obvious is that the bear was said to have formidable strength. The second is the fact that this particular bear was blind.

Another unpalatable custom of the period was that some of the fiercest bears had their eyes put out, in order to give the dogs a fighting chance. In the case of Samson, the men charged with the task had successfully blinded him in the left eye and done what they reckoned to be a reasonable job on the right, whereas, in fact, much of their work on the latter had been inflicted on the flesh around it, so that the bear managed to retain some sight. But from that point on in order to look about him Samson was obliged to turn his whole head, which made him appear a little dim-witted and may well have contributed to his appeal.

The bear's reputation went before it. He was a monster, smashing and rending apart every dog that came his way, despite the fact that his head and hindquarters were a mass of scars, half his fur was missing and one ear had been completely chewed away. Then, quite suddenly, it seemed that at every appearance the stands were packed, with hundreds more being refused entry. And in a matter of months the public's adoration had grown so strong that it was decided to take him out of service, before some new dog got its teeth into an artery and killed him, whereupon, it was thought, there would have been some sort of insurrection and half the city razed to the ground.

So in early April the bear was formally granted a pardon. And for the whole of that summer he toured the pits and gardens, where he was paraded and encouraged to raise a paw to give the crowd its blessing – a salute solemnly returned by every spectator. But despite the fact that Samson had retired from fighting, the crowds kept growing – if only to catch one last glimpse of the legendary bear. There seemed to be no bounds to its popularity so, in order to draw a line under the whole affair, it was suggested that the bear be officially honoured by being presented with the key to the city, then sent out of London for good.

There was talk of releasing the bear out in Epping, or building some special Bear House upriver where people could pay to ogle at him from a boat. In truth, several men of significant standing privately felt that everyone's lives would be made a lot less complicated if they could only despatch the blasted bear, without anyone knowing, and spread some story that it had been put out to pasture in Northumberland or some other part of the country where people rarely went.

But before any decision was made regarding Samson's 'retirement' there was the matter of the key to the city, which was to be presented by the Lord Mayor himself. Out at Spitalfields a vast stage was constructed and people began bagging prime spots three clear days before the event. On the Friday night it is estimated ten thousand Londoners slept under the stars in the vicinity. By eight o'clock on the Saturday morning thirty-five thousand packed into the fields, carried along on a wave of bear-worship (and the fact that there was nothing much else happening that weekend).

Samson finally arrived, down Hog Lane, around ten o'clock, its paws chained together before it, and a second chain fitted between its wrists and the halter round its neck. It had an escort of a dozen or so men, as much for

its own protection as that of the public. In fact, Samson was becoming accustomed to a somewhat cosseted lifestyle. Over the last few months those people in charge of his welfare had detected what they felt was a distinct mellowing in the bear's attitude. He was, after all, well-fed, had comfortable sleeping arrangements and was used to having his meals served at regular intervals.

The first cheers came up from the hundred or so spectators who'd climbed up into the treetops as they caught sight of the bear and his escorts heading towards the back of the stage. And as soon as they started up everyone else began craning their necks and jostling one another and the pandemonium grew from there. When the bear stepped out onto the platform the whole crowd surged forward. A good proportion of them had been up all night, drinking and singing, and would have had some trouble identifying their own husbands and wives. But they knew that bear – the famous bear with the one ear and the one good eye. So they began chanting its name and clapping and stamping. And generally helped drum up an atmosphere which was so exceptional in its raucous good nature that, even if there was nothing better all day

than this very moment, they thought, then it would have been worth it just the same.

The uproar continued unabated for a good five minutes. Meanwhile the bear just stood and looked out from the stage. Finally, some official stepped forward and tried to get the crowd to quieten down, so that the Lord Mayor might be able to deliver his speech. But the crowd just kept on bawling and chanting, and waving at the bear, until the official eventually turned and strode over to the Lord Mayor and suggested, by cupping his hands over one ear and shouting into it, that as there didn't appear to be much prospect of the crowd calming down in the immediate future, he might consider scrapping the speech and cutting straight to the handing-over-of-the-key.

The Lord Mayor was a tad disappointed. He'd seen this as an opportunity to ingratiate himself with the common man and woman (and from what he could see of them, the majority of the crowd spread out before him were very common indeed). All the same, he made his way to the front of the stage, as directed, and Samson's minders encouraged the great bear to take up a position next to him.

The Lord Mayor had already come to the conclusion that, considering the colossal audience, it was probably best to present the highlight of the ceremony with the broadest of strokes. So he took the key from his pocket, held it up and turned to east and west so that everyone could see it, like a magician setting up some sleight of hand. Then, in a highly exaggerated fashion, he turned and offered the key to the bear.

Samson leant forward and peered at the key for a couple of moments. It was newly minted and glinted in the sun. The bear glanced up at the face of the fellow offering it, then picked the key cleanly out of the Lord Mayor's palm, without hesitation, as if he was handed keys every day of the week. The Lord Mayor turned to the row of dignitaries standing behind him, who were all nodding and smiling. It had been a lot easier than they thought it was going to be.

Samson transferred the key to his left paw, studied it with his one good eye, sniffed it, and deduced quite quickly that whatever it was, it was probably not edible. But at this point the Lord Mayor made his fatal error. He saw how the bear's right paw was free. And, thinking that a handshake might be appropriate, as if to seal the deal, he reached out and took the bear's chained paw.

He hoped that this image of man and bear in brotherly union would stay in people's minds. Indeed, it would. That moment and all the moments which followed would be imprinted on the memories of everyone who witnessed them right through their lives. Samson took the Lord Mayor's right hand and locked its paw around it. With its other paw it took hold of his right arm. It was a grip of tremendous conviction. And when the Lord Mayor looked into the bear's one good eye he saw terrible things there.

'It's going to rip my arm right out of its socket,' he

thought to himself. 'It's going to rip my arm out of its socket and toss it to the crowd.'

He merely underestimated the bear's ambitions. Samson turned, skipped to the left and brought the Lord Mayor around behind him, so that both the fellow's feet left the ground. And once the Lord Mayor had reached optimum height and velocity, the bear let him go.

The Mayor went sailing out over the heads of his fellow-Londoners. If they had felt for him even a fraction of the affection they had been expressing for the bear they might have tried to catch him, or made some effort to try and break his fall. Instead, at the very last moment,

when it was evident whereabouts he was going to land, they parted, leaving a clearing just wide enough to accommodate him.

As he hit the ground a collective '*Ohhhh*' went up from the spectators. Some turned away; some covered their faces. Others went up onto tiptoe, to try to get a better view. But people were not yet running and screaming. They were biding their time and wondering what tricks the bear might get up to next.

The moment the Lord Mayor went flying, all the other dignitaries scurried off into the wings, so that Samson soon had the stage to himself. He stood and surveyed the city – out past the spires and the smoking chimney pots. Then he dropped his head, like an actor preparing for a particularly demanding soliloquy.

The bear filled its lungs, brought both paws up before it, and slowly raised its head. An awful grimace was spread across it. And the crowd saw how the bear drew its paws out towards its shoulders . . . and how the chain that held them took the strain.

The crowd was entranced, and for the first time in several days a stillness fell across the fields. Samson rolled its head right back, teeth bared, to face the sun. And those down at the front were able to see how a single link in the middle of the chain slowly opened. Until, finally, it flew off, the chain split, and the bear's arms were free.

The audience was half-inclined to cheer such a specta-cle – but something stopped them. Something held them back. Samson studied the crowd quite coldly. Then filled its lungs again. And this time, instead of holding its breath, to generate the strength required to break its chains, the bear opened its great jaw and all that power came flooding out.

A staggering roar rolled across the city . . . raced up the river . . . swept down every lane and alleyway. And after a moment, in the silence that followed, other roars came rolling back in. One came up from Saffron Hill . . . one from Toothill . . . another from out at Hockley-in-the-Hole. Every bear in the city was calling out now. The roars grew louder and more persistent. And it was at this point that the crowd felt a sudden and powerful inclination to be somewhere else.

The stage had been built to a height of twenty feet, to allow as many Londoners as possible to witness the ceremony and to discourage them from attempting to climb up onto it. But Samson was down off it in next to no time. People suddenly started moving. In a matter of seconds the ground before the stage was cleared, save for the Lord Mayor's mangled body, like a drowned man, revealed by the tide's retreat.

As Samson advanced people began tripping and falling. Began to be trampled underfoot. And when they headed into the streets and those same streets narrowed, the crowd heaved and surged like a mindless animal, until the bodies began to collect, compressed and breathless, and the rest turned back and went charging off a different way.

Here and there, the bear stopped to pick up some scrap of food, dropped in the melee. For the first time in his life Samson was entirely free from chains. And as he made his way down Houndsditch he roared again, and a hundred roars came echoing back towards him, as the city's bear population began to rally, began to come to life.

Down at Bankside a dozen bears heaved at the bars of their cages until the cement finally cracked and crumbled and they went charging out into the streets. And every

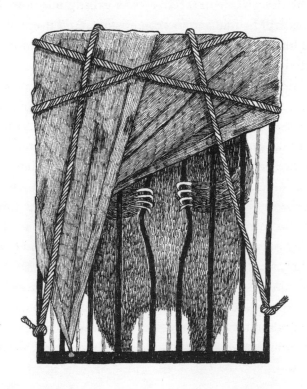

bear from Aldgate all the way over to Long Acre took hold of the bars and they too started heaving at them, their strength suddenly doubled now that the roars of all the free bears filled their ears. As each bear broke out it joined forces with the others and together they followed the roars of those bears still imprisoned and set about liberating them, until some bear-jailers panicked and threw the doors open, in the hope that their bears might go off and lay waste to some other part of the city and that they might be spared.

The bears roamed the streets in great packs, broken chains still hanging from their wrists and halters. And the blinded bears came up into the daylight, led by the sighted bears. The dogs barked, then ran for cover. The cats hid wherever they could. And people dashed here and there, frantically looking for husbands, wives and children, as the bears toured the streets of this new London. And anyone foolish enough to try to obstruct them was swept away.

The Londoners retreated into their homes, then up into their attics and finally out onto the rooftops, where they had a grandstand view of their neighbourhood being ripped apart. For three whole days the bears ruled the city. On the Sunday the infantry were sent in to try and impose some sort of order, but within a couple of hours they were chased back out.

Bear-anarchy was firmly established and people began to wonder how many weeks or months the bears might prevail. But on the Tuesday morning the city woke to find the streets deserted. The roars had subsided soon after midnight, but no one dared investigate until the sun was well and truly up. When they finally crept out it seemed as if every pane of glass in the city had been shattered – not just those in the shops, but in every house and church and inn. Furniture had been dragged out and homes ransacked. Horses wandered, wild-eyed. Rats flitted between the debris. But the bears were gone.

In the weeks which followed there was the odd report of a gang of bears seen on the move, upcountry – the first on the outskirts of Oxford, another just south of Manchester. Then nothing. And it was widely assumed that the bears had either set up shop in another part of the country or simply starved to death. For the people of London, either outcome would have been quite acceptable.

But essentially that was the end of bear-baiting and bear-pits and bear-gardens. Perhaps, some Londoners thought, it was for the best. All the same, as they swept up the mess and salvaged what little they could from the wreckage, they were inclined to wonder how they might be expected to entertain themselves now – now that their bear-sport had been suspended and the bears had had their sport with them.

4

Circus Bears

It was a time of elasticated ladies – a time of human cannonballs. Right across the land, men were swallowing swords, setting themselves on fire, being bundled into sacks and thrown into the sea. Women were tying themselves in knots, having knives thrown at them and, in any time they had left over, juggling budgerigars.

If you were unusually tall or short or ugly, or had bits missing or, indeed, had supplementary bits, then there was money to be made – if not necessarily *by* you, then on your behalf. If you happened to be a woman with a beard or a cleft palate, or a fellow with a good-sized goitre or especially scaly skin then the general public would queue up outside your allotted tent and hand over their hard-earned money to have a closer look at you.

And just as the public would queue to see unusual-looking humans, they also liked nothing better than to see wild animals strut and stroll just like one of us. So there were learned pigs, and dogs dressed as infants and monkey-acrobats. There were mathematical horses, seal-musicians and, inevitably, there were performing bears.

Roughly forty bears were employed in England's fairs and circuses. No one could quite recall, or frankly cared, where they originated. The bears themselves had no strong opinion on the matter. Any memory of their ancestral home had been shaken out of them as they clung to a horse as it galloped round the ring's perimeter, or been burnt away in the heat of the spotlight as they prepared to step out onto the high-wire. Whatever variety of bear they had once been was now irrelevant. Their masters saw them only as circus bears and, in truth, that was how most of the bears saw themselves.

It was a hard life but earlier bears had had it harder. Generally speaking, circus bears were not too frequently beaten, and only killed if they'd behaved especially badly or reached the age when they were of no further use. The odd hank of meat was tossed into their cages most evenings. And some bears developed quite a powerful bond with those men and women who looked after them.

Frank Boswell was the animal trainer with a small touring circus and, as such, had in his charge a rather crotchety old bear called Mr Fowler. Frank Boswell was not a well man. To put it bluntly, Frank was a drunk. He had always taken his drinking more seriously than other people, but in recent years had hit the bottle so early in the morning and carried on so late after the show that it was hard to tell when one day's drinking ended and the next day's boozing began.

Late one night Mr Fowler woke to find old Frank peering in through the bars of his cage. Mr Fowler had the feeling that he'd been there for quite some time. As Mr Fowler watched, Boswell took his keys and undid the cage's padlock. Then he led the old bear out into the night.

Mr Fowler wasn't sure what was happening. To be fair, the old bear was still half-asleep. It was too late in the day, the bear reasoned, to be learning a new routine. Too late

in the day in all sorts of ways. Frank brought a finger up to his lips and led him between the caravans and out into a meadow. It was summer and the air was warm and still. Frank stared out over the moonlit fields. Mr Fowler studied his trainer with not the slightest idea what was going on inside of him. He seemed to have drifted off into some drunken reverie. When he finally re-surfaced the old man turned and looked up at Mr Fowler, then began undoing the bear's remaining chains.

'I'm sorry,' old Frank insisted. He might have been crying. 'I should've done this years ago.'

The bear rubbed his wrists and looked about him. And for a while, man and bear just stood beside each other in the warm summer's night. Mr Fowler didn't seem to properly appreciate what was expected of him and after a minute or so Frank was obliged to give him a gentle push, to set him on his way. The bear took a single, hesitant step. He wasn't used to being out at such an hour. The bear was baffled. His trainer pointed across the meadow towards the trees in the distance. The bear began to shuffle off in that direction, then stopped and looked back at the man who'd been his constant companion for all these years. Frank pointed again, to encourage the beast to get a move-on. But something was stopping the bear. It dropped its head and shuffled back over to Frank – towered over him. Slipped both paws around his shoulders and drew the old man into him.

'I shall miss you, Mr Fowler,' Frank told the bear. 'You have been like a friend to me.'

The bear continued to embrace him, as if, now that he was on the verge of freedom, he was in two minds as to whether he had the courage to go.

'Mr Fowler,' the old trainer whispered. 'You're . . . *hurting . . . me.*'

But Mr Fowler just kept on squeezing – kept on squeezing until, one by one, the trainer's ribs began to

pop. The bear kept on. Couldn't help itself. Kept on squeezing until the last of Frank's drunken breath was gone. When it finally released its grip Frank Boswell dropped to the ground like a sack of potatoes. Mr Fowler stood and looked down at him for a while. Then he turned and headed across the meadows. As he went, he glanced up at the night sky. By Mr Fowler's reckoning, he still had a good three or four hours before dawn.

The authorities finally caught up with Mr Fowler late the following morning and promptly hanged him. Just threw a rope up into the nearest tree capable of taking a bear's weight and strung him up for all the world to see. This was a little unnecessary, considering the bear had been knocked down and killed by a carriage a good three hours earlier. Hanging him was a sort of belated retribution for the death of Frank Boswell. It was also, in its way, intended as a warning to other bears.

And word certainly got around the other circuses. People who'd barely heard of Boswell suddenly claimed to have been on the most intimate terms with him, and the few qualities he'd had to recommend him became so wildly exaggerated that overnight he was transformed into such a paragon of honour and decency that those folk who really did know him thought that people must have been talking about somebody else. But the repercussions of Frank's death were also felt in human–bear relations. And there's no doubt that bear welfare (which wasn't of the highest standard to begin with) suffered a significant dip.

The bears were already deeply disgruntled at all the

extra risks being incorporated into their performance. It was no longer sufficient for a bear to walk the high-wire with an open umbrella. They were now obliged to carry a suitcase and wear a two-piece suit as well. The suit was specially tailored for them, with buttons down both sides for easy fitting and removal, but it was still an added hindrance. Bears in one touring circus were regularly kitted out in skirts and dresses, with bonnets tied to their head. There was even talk of training bears in some of the trapeze work. The bears did not like the sound of that at all.

When they'd started out the bears had carried the pole across their chest, just like any high-wire walker. The trainer's only objective had been to get them across without incident. But as soon as the bears were competent, the pole was removed and ever since there seemed to have been an unspoken policy to have the bears appear more and more ridiculous.

Only six months earlier, a bear had taken a tumble. It had been dressed up like a mountain climber, with a coil of rope across one shoulder and a canvas rucksack on its back. One of the boys had pulled the straps too tight when fitting the rucksack and, halfway over, the bear had twisted its shoulder, just to loosen it off a bit. It lost its footing and fell fifty feet onto the sawdust. For ten long minutes it just lay there, writhing and groaning, until someone managed to track down Bob Welland, who was known to own a rifle and he finally arrived and put the creature out of its misery. There was a cursory effort to sanitise proceedings by having a few lads hold up blankets. But there was no mistaking the gunshot when it rang out.

A day or two later, one of the broom boys claimed to have caught a pair of bears 'communicating' late at night, through the bars of their cages. As he passed by, he said, the bears suddenly fell silent and just watched him until he was out of the way. Even then, it was suggested, seeds of dissent had been sown and the whiff of conspiracy was in the air.

Horace Maddigan liked to set himself apart from the hoi polloi in all sorts of ways, but one or two in particular. Professionally, Maddigan's Family Butchers had earned him a seat at the top table of Bristol's Chamber of Commerce, and privately Horace had a bit of a thing for circuses. Like everyone else, he delighted in the apparent barely controlled chaos, but he also had romantic ideas about the exotic company and the rough-and-ready way of life. Falling asleep at night, he liked to pretend that he was tucked up in a caravan, with a long day's drive ahead of him and an acrobatic wife at his side who, with a little encouragement, was capable of putting both ankles behind her neck.

One Tuesday evening, after a meeting of local businessmen, and for the only time in his life Horace allowed the personal to get tangled up with the professional when he got to talking with a couple of other fellows about his dream of staging the country's first circus convention. And through a combination of rare Scotch whiskies and tales of wild goings-on involving circus women, he somehow managed to infect his companions' addled minds with his own delusions, and to such a profound degree, that the three of them made a pact, there and then, and over the next eighteen months devoted their every spare hour to plotting and scheming until they managed to drag Horace Maddigan's dream into reality.

For the whole of May the fields out by Ashton Court were packed with big tops. Many of the circus workers and performers were well acquainted. Some were old friends, which led to some serious drinking sessions, one or two of which got out of hand and necessitated the calling out of the local constabulary. There were also a few long-standing rivalries and instances of bad blood, which occasionally boiled-over and necessitated calling out the constabulary again. But on the whole the houses were full, or near enough, and it seemed that the people of Bristol and the surrounding villages were only too willing to hike up the hill and pay to see a different circus every night of the week.

The whole event was due to finish on the last Saturday of May and the organisers were quietly confident of turning a decent profit. But the events on the Wednesday saw to that . . .

In the main tent the evening had started out quite promisingly with some bare-backed horse-riding, a little clowning and tumbling and plenty of crashing of cymbals and other musical distractions to cover up the cracks. Then the MC stepped into the follow-spot, did a little patter and threw out his left arm. And the light swung around and flooded the tunnel, as the bear came hurtling into the ring.

The bear's entrance was greeted with unanimous approval. Most of the audience had never seen a live bear before and the fact that it was pedalling a tricycle, just like some big fellow strapped into a bear-suit, had the crowd in stitches and slapping their thighs with delight. It was ridiculous. In all sorts of ways it was ridiculous. Down at the front, some young boy watched, bewildered. 'That bear's too big for that bicycle,' he thought to himself.

But the tiny wheels only made the bear pedal that much faster. The poor bear was pedalling like billy-o. On a typical night he would do a couple of circuits, jump off his bike, have his gown removed by an assistant and, with only the occasional prod of encouragement from his trainer, make his way over to the ladder and up to the wire. But the bear just kept on pedalling. He did an extra circuit, then another one on top of that. Up in the band, the trumpet-player looked over at the drummer. The two of them just shrugged and, like the bear, went around again. By now, even some members of the audience sensed that something was the matter. This bear-on-a-tricycle lark was running out of steam. One fellow was thinking to himself, 'He should jump off his bike and maybe do some juggling. Or grab some lady from the audience and shake her up a bit.'

But the bear persisted with the pedalling. In fact, it appeared to be pedalling even harder than before. Then, suddenly, it dropped its shoulder, leaned to the left and headed for the tunnel. The spotlight followed him and picked out the MC in the shadows, having a drag on a cigarillo. He shielded his eyes as the light engulfed him and before he even saw it, the bear was past him and carrying on its way.

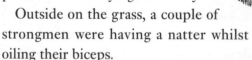

Outside on the grass, a couple of strongmen were having a natter whilst oiling their biceps.

'Stop him,' someone shouted from the big top. 'Stop the bear.'

They only had a couple of moments in which to make a decision but it was long enough to detect something unforgiving in the bear's attitude, and despite all their collective muscle they ultimately chose to skip out of the way.

All around the tent stood a six-foot fence, obliging the bear to head for the gate beside the ticket office where a few young lads were hanging around. They heard a bit of a commotion and turned in time to see the bear come hammering towards them, with the MC and the strongmen jogging along behind. But when the bear was no more than four or five yards from them, he bared his teeth and let out an almighty roar. And in that instant the way was made clear and the bear flew past them and pedalled out into the crowd.

That roar focussed the attention of every soul within two hundred paces. The punters milling among the tents saw a cycling bear go weaving between them and assumed that this was an extra bit of entertainment they were getting for free. The bear steered in and out of them, until some clear space finally appeared up ahead. Then it caught the evening air in its nostrils and found itself pedalling down an open road.

If the first roar had got the other bears' attention, the second was like a call to arms. They suddenly understood that the bear was moving . . . was in charge of its own progress . . . and that they must follow. And that no chain or trainer could stand in their way.

Fifty yards down the lane the bear finally abandoned its tricycle, which was just as well as a gang of showfolk wasn't far behind and were short on ideas as to what they might do if they actually caught up with him. But this group of pursuers soon found themselves being overtaken by the other bears, which they found a little unnerving. Most of the bears were still in costume – dressed in dinner jackets and pyjamas and petticoats. When the bears came alongside, the showfolk slackened their pace a little. Then, once the bears had passed, they checked over their shoulder to make sure there were no more coming, and slowly picked up speed again.

Further back, a second wave of people came running: more circus workers, along with over a hundred punters, including a number of children. Only one man had had the foresight, before setting off, to consider a scenario in which a bear might actually be cornered.

'Find Bob Welland,' he called out to a young lad, before leaving. 'And tell him to fetch his gun.'

Bob was quickly located and now came along at the rear of the second pack. But Bob was a decent runner and it wasn't long before he was at the front of the second mob and gaining on the mob up ahead.

The bears hadn't a clue where they were going – were just pleased to be out in the open air. They'd stretched their limbs more in the last five minutes than they'd done in the previous five years. They were in a great gang now, but had no leader. They just followed the lane as it swept down the avenue. But as they pressed on the quality of the terrain began to deteriorate, until it was nothing but an unmade road. And then they were leaping over signs and wooden fences, and passing piles of earth and stacks of posts.

It was someone in the second group who first appreci-ated their impending predicament. 'The bears,' he called out. 'They're heading straight for the bridge.'

In point of fact, to describe it in such terms was some way short of accurate. The groundwork had commenced a good three years earlier and the huge towers at each side of the gorge were now complete. The cables which would ultimately hold the structure together had been hung between them. But it would be another year or more before the road itself was suspended and any vehicles or pedestrians would make their way across. So, in the conventional sense, it was far from being a bridge.

By the time the first crowd of people rounded the corner the bears were already clambering up the scaffolding and gathering at the top of the tower. Two great cables hung over the gorge like giant skipping ropes. It was a two-hundred-and-fifty-foot drop to the treetops and river below.

The audience just stood and watched as the first bear stepped onto one of the cables. Inching forward, it reached out a paw to left and right, just as it did on the high-wire. A second bear slowly stepped onto the other cable. And within a minute all the bears were edging out over the gorge in two long lines.

The second group of pursuers had arrived now and stood and gaped alongside the others. And perhaps they would've done nothing more, until all the bears had completed the crossing, if a small child hadn't broken the silence.

'They're getting away,' he said.

Bob Welland was ushered forward. The crowd made way for him. They watched as he positioned himself, swallowed hard and brought the rifle up to his shoulder.

He closed one eye and focussed on a bear in the

middle. Picked it out because of its petticoats. He slowly followed it as it slid each paw forward. Saw nothing else now – just the bear in the petticoats and, beyond it, the woods on the far side of the gorge.

But as he held his breath and focussed, he suddenly thought, 'Honest to God. What on earth am I *doing*?' Then, 'Even if I manage to hit one bear, it's not as if all the rest would suddenly turn around.'

As far as Bob was concerned he'd already shot one bear, and that was one too many. At this rate they'd be carving 'Bob Welland, Killer of Bears' on his headstone.

Bob opened his other eye, breathed out, and brought the gun down, which was met with some confusion. Most of the children had their fingers in their ears, ready for the gunshot. Bob was shaking his head.

'I'm sorry,' he said.

But the man standing next to him was the general manager of one of the circuses. He'd paid good money for his bears, not to mention all the training and feeding. And whilst he may not have held out any more hope than Bob of actually retrieving his assets he sure as hell wasn't going to stand around and just watch them get away.

'Give it 'ere,' he said.

He snatched the gun from Bob's hands, brought it up and squeezed the trigger. Given that he barely bothered to take aim the results were quite spectacular. There was a distant but audible clang as bullet struck metal and the bear in the petticoat seemed to stall, twist, then tip to one side.

The same child who, a minute before, had broken the silence by pointing out that the bears were escaping, piped up again.

'He got one,' he said.

In fact, the man with the rifle had done no such thing. He'd merely clipped a steel link which gripped the cables a clear yard to the right of one of the bears, but it was enough to break its concentration. And making the bear jump had set in motion any number of twists and turns, as it endeavoured to correct itself. Until its final act was to reach down and try to grab the cable. It got within half an inch. Its claws brushed the air just above it. Then the bear started to fall.

It fell head first. In the crowd, mothers covered their children's faces. Others averted their eyes. As the bear fell, it slowly turned, executing a cartwheel in mid-air. But when it was more or less upright, something peculiar happened. From a distance it looked like a small explosion of clothing. The bear's skirts suddenly caught the upward draught, billowed and locked into place. And the bear's descent was reduced, from that of a falling boulder to a gentle drift.

As long as the bear held its paws out over its dresses to stop them flapping up around its ears that gentle drift continued, and by carefully leaning to left and right it discovered that it could, to some extent, control its flight.

An old man was walking his dog along the bank of the river. He'd heard the to-do, had looked up to see some people climbing out over the cables and heard the gunshot. Had seen some lady fall, and for almost a minute, nothing but frilly underwear, as she sailed towards him. She landed about twenty yards up the shore, then proceeded to rip all her clothes off, including her bonnet, whereupon the old fellow suddenly appreciated that she was actually a bear. The bear turned, gave him a rather sinister look, then ran off, in the opposite direction. Man and dog just stood and stared, dumbstruck. Then they both looked up again, to see if any more were on their way.

The other bears turned their attention back to their high-wire walking. All their training, it seemed, had not been in vain. The trickiest part was the ascent from the dip in the middle to the tower on the other side. But once the first two or three had completed the crossing they waited and offered encouragement to those that came behind.

No more shots echoed up and down the gorge that day. And it wasn't long before the final bear teetered along the last few yards of cable and joined the rest of the bears.

There was a moment, once the bears were re-united, when they looked back at their audience. Instinctively, a young girl raised her hand. And soon, all the children in the crowd were gently waving, like some private salutation. But the bears didn't respond. They just turned their backs and within a couple of moments had disappeared from view.

5

Sewer Bears

We all have our dark little secrets – those sources of shame which make us flinch whenever they come to mind. So it is with every town and city. And none more so than the city of London, which has enough skeletons in its cupboards to keep the whole place a-rattling from now till Kingdom Come.

One of its guiltiest secrets is that, for a good proportion of the nineteenth century, bears were kept locked in its sewers, where they served as the city's unpaid flushers and toshers. Around a hundred bears patrolled that stinking labyrinth of pipe and tunnel which carried away the waste from the city's homes and factories, and drained the water from the streets. Without their efforts every heavy rainfall would have plunged the whole place underwater and the air would have been thick with pestilence.

But make no mistake, the bears were prisoners. Every grate and manhole cover was locked tight-shut. The only light that found its way down to them was that which filtered through the grates and gulleys, or came up from the gates where the drains emptied straight into the Thames.

It was the bears' unenviable task to accompany the city's effluvia, from the moment it first entered the system right down to the river. True, gravity bore some of that burden. But it is in the nature of sewage to coalesce at every opportunity, to silt-up at every turn. The bears' only objective was to keep things moving. For they knew that, whatever they managed to clear before them, there would always be plenty more coming along behind.

Bears were regularly carried away in the throes of a flash-flood. To try and guard against such an eventuality they constructed a series of ledges – shadowy recesses high up in the brickwork, to which they could retreat whenever the levels suddenly rose. Even so, every hour of labour was carried out in fearful anticipation of a downpour. If the drains were not sufficiently clear they knew the sewage would rise – and keep on rising – and no matter where the bears were hiding the flood would eventually find them out.

All in all, it was a sorry sort of existence. Their only nourishment came from whatever edible scraps they happened to find about them, or acquired by trading those few items of value they turned up during the day. The sewers beneath the breweries and slaughter-houses were significant stations on their circuits, but were just as popular with every other creature trying to survive

64

underground. On the whole, rats were more wary of bears than vice-versa, and, if necessary, the bears were quite prepared to make a meal of them. But the rats were quick, and capable of delivering a nasty nip before departing so, by and large, bear and rat left each other to their own individual brand of misery – or as much as was possible in the circumstances.

The bears operated in gangs, each team despatched to a particular precinct, with their makeshift rods and shovels to prise the foul matter from where it had set. They worked in shifts, moving in as soon as possible after someone had shot the night soil or deposited a tank or two of offal, whatever time of night or day that might happen to be.

A century later, long after the bears had abandoned the tunnels, a group of academics, investigating the bears' subterranean existence, discovered great expanses of wall, decorated with a multitude of tiny scratches, which they interpreted, quite wrongly, as bear-hieroglyphics . . . something akin to the primitive cave drawings in France and southern Spain. But there was nothing remotely artistic about them. They were simply a means for the bears to mark off those parts of the city which had been visited and the distribution of bear-labour on any given day.

The concentration of so many pestilential and poison-ous gases meant there was always a risk of explosion and, from time to time, some errant spark would set the whole lot off. The authorities took a philosophical view on the matter, being of the opinion that, as long as such explosions were kept below ground and didn't injure anybody of import, then they were to be tolerated. So it wasn't unusual for Londoners to hear a muted thump and register a minor tremor through their shoe leather as some hideous combination of gases, long compressed between the brickwork, finally found the ignition it craved.

In the summer of 1849 the pavements of John Street, just off Gray's Inn Road, unexpectedly erupted and, soon after, two bears were seen climbing out between the flags. They got as far as Red Lion Park where they climbed up into the trees. Marksmen were brought in and both bears were shot and killed. Their bodies were taken away and disposed of, and those passers-by who happened to witness the incident were encouraged to keep it to themselves.

The bears lived in constant fear of such explosions and did everything in their power to prevent them coming about, but they also knew that such an event offered their only chance of freedom, so whenever a sewer did go up they would rush to the scene, partly to see if any bear had been injured, but also carrying with them some faint hope that their moment of liberation might have finally arrived.

The odd explosion, along with the general wear and tear of the tunnels, necessitated a certain degree of maintenance beyond the bears' abilities, and the men who undertook these brief ventures into the underworld did

so with the same level of wariness as a sortie behind enemy lines. Among those employed to do such work, stories were rife of men who'd failed to watch their backs and been dragged off into the darkness.

'They loves human flesh,' one fellow was fond of saying. 'To bears, we tastes just like chicken.' Although how he happened to come by such particular information was never made clear.

It is impossible to estimate what number of Londoners knew of the bears' existence. Certainly, no committees were formed to lobby for an improvement in their conditions, and no Member of Parliament got to his feet to call for their release. The best that can be said is that it was a subject on which most people chose not to dwell.

The only Londoners to have regular contact with the bears were the Gutter Traders, an informal association of no more than twenty men in all. As already stated, the bears would gather on their rounds a certain amount of edible matter (if that is not too exaggerated a claim for it) as well as any odds and ends which might have some value to those citizens up above. The simple fact is that the bears lived their lives in a state of perpetual hunger. In order to avoid starvation they developed a means of exchanging any knick-knack they had found or the odd coin or piece of jewellery for some morsel of food which might help sustain them and their fellow-bears through another day.

At dawn, it was not unusual to find some seedy-looking character kneeling at the kerbside, apparently conversing with a drain. Every now and again they would slip their fingers through the grate and pick something out. Then bring it up to their face and examine it, sometimes with the aid of an eyeglass. There would follow a period of negotiation. Finally, some package of meat or bag of left-overs would be deposited. Then the dealer would take up his latest acquisitions and go on his way.

The system was far from perfect, but worked well enough for both parties to persist with it. Any Trader who drove too hard a bargain would find themselves avoided. If the bears were too demanding they would go without.

In such negotiations the Trader did all the talking. If the deal was considered unacceptable, the bear would shake its head. Then it was up to the Trader to restate his position, or amend his terms. Some deal was usually struck. And, to be fair, it was a rare day when there was anything like outright hostility, which was due in no small part to the fate suffered by a local character known as Jimmy the Hat.

Jimmy got his name on account of his rather beaten old bowler that he was said to have picked out of the gutter. He'd been dealing with the bears for no more than a fort-night and was there early one morning, at the usual grate. A couple of bits and pieces were passed up: bent cutlery, some sort of buckle and so on, none of which had made much impression.

'Anythin' else?' said Jimmy.

The bear studied Jimmy for a second, apparently

uncertain as to whether to proceed. Then slowly
unfolded a grubby old rag. A gold ring sat in it. Jimmy
could see it glinting just below the bars and he knew, even
at that distance, that it was worth something. He could
feel it in his bones.

The ring had a stone set in it, which caught a small
fraction of light. 'Pass it up,' he said.

The bear was reluctant to hand the ring over – had
spent enough years sifting through the filth and trading
the few things that were to be salvaged from it to appreciate that this was not your average find.

Jimmy the Hat was all shrugs and open palms. 'I've got
to have a proper look,' he said, 'to see if there's any
maker's marks on it.'

The bear didn't have much choice, and eventually the
ring went up through the bars, just as it must have once
slipped down between them, except this time it was held
between the claws of a bear. Jimmy took it and brought it

up to his eye. And even as he did so, he was already getting to his feet and glancing over his shoulder, as if to find the light. When he was standing he had one more look at the ring, then calmly slipped it in his waistcoat pocket. Then he winked at the bear beneath the bars, turned, and walked away.

The bear let out a great roar from its dungeon, but Jimmy was already scuttling off down the street. The bear roared again and pressed its nose right up against the cold metal, to try and get one last sniff of Jimmy – to draw in the man's rancid smell and hold it there.

There was nothing to be done. The other bears were informed of the situation and told to keep an eye out for the evil little shyster. And for the next few months the cheated bear went out of its way to work in those neighbourhoods that a swindler such as Jimmy the Hat might frequent.

The weeks went by. One Trader said he'd heard how much Jimmy had sold the ring for – enough to feed the

bears for well over a month. Another said he had it on good authority that Jimmy had upped sticks and headed west. The other bears turned their attention back to their clearing and shovelling, but at night the cheated bear would lie on its ledge and relive every dreadful second until its whole body burned and ached.

Then one day, quite out of the blue, Jimmy was spotted over in Whitechapel, outside the old Cock and Bottle, having had an ale or two too many and been thrown out for causing a scene. The bear he'd robbed was informed and was over there in a matter of minutes. Managed to clamber up a drain and get its snout right up to street level.

The bear drew in a deep draught of the East End evening. And in among the hundred other smells, it could clearly pick out that thieving beggar, Jimmy the Hat. The bear pulled back its head, twisted itself round and got a shoulder right up into the culvert. It could hear Jimmy now, sounding off to a taxi driver, and a few moments later insulting a woman who happened to be walking by.

A boot stepped down into the gutter and was soon joined by its twin. The feet shuffled as they did their best to keep their owner upright. Jimmy was about to head off across the road, but at the last second was obliged to stop as some carriage went flying past him. The bear heard Jimmy curse the driver. Then it reached out and made a grab for him.

The carriage was gone. Jimmy had finished his

shouting. He set off. But something was stopping him – something interfered. He thought perhaps he'd got his boot caught up on something, but when he looked down he saw a great paw clamped round his ankle. Jimmy had drunk many beers and several whiskies, but in that instant he became as sober as a judge.

He tried to tug his leg away, but it wasn't moving. He tried to kick at the paw with his other foot but the bear didn't mind a bit. Jimmy dropped down into the gutter and tried undoing his laces. It would be worth the loss of a boot, he thought. But every time he went anywhere near the laces the bear just shifted its grip, until it had a hold of his shin instead.

Jimmy began calling out to passers-by to help him – the same passers-by he'd been abusing only minutes before. Most of them just ignored him. The rest took one look at the situation and decided not to get involved.

With every minute, Jimmy was getting more and more frantic. Below, the bear could smell the bitter panic in his sweat. The other bears gathered round and offered to help – to try and get a hold of the other boot, or to take over for a minute – but all offers were refused. There was only one possible set of circumstances in which the bear would ever consider releasing its grip.

After half an hour or so, Jimmy collapsed, through sheer nervous exhaustion. This was probably not advisable. For one thing, it allowed the bear to drag his foot deeper into the culvert. For another, it allowed the bear to get a good look at him. Jimmy saw the bear's eye glinting in the darkness. The bear saw the same eye that had winked at him before making off with that precious ring.

It isn't true that Jimmy was eaten alive. It is one of those little legends which seem to gain credence with the passing of time. The fact is that once the bear got enough of Jimmy's leg down into the gutter, it took a bite or two – just to get him bleeding. After that, the bear was quite happy to hold on and let all the life slowly drain out of him.

For the last hour of his life Jimmy had quite an audience – they stood on the other side of the street, not saying a word. Just watching, as Jimmy went through one or two periods in which he made quite a fuss and squealed and thrashed about like a trapped animal. Then periods when he grew quite still.

When he was finally dead the bears dragged the body down into the sewers with them. Bears are practical creatures and will make use of whatever meat happens to be lying around, which is probably where the stories of Jimmy being eaten alive have their origins. He went down bit by bit, until with one last tug Jimmy's head disappeared into the darkness and all that remained in the gutter was his battered bowler, less than quarter of a mile from where he'd first picked it up.

For the bears, Jimmy's comeuppance was a significant victory, but all too soon the daily grind reimposed itself, and the idea of Jimmy held by his ankle began to recede.

And it was back to the old routine of trudge and sludge, with just an occasional breather. Then sleep, high up among the brickwork, as if the bears were a part of the city's very soil.

At each day's end the bears would gather by the main gate, where the passage widened before disgorging its contents into the river. Twenty or thirty bears would sometimes sit and stare out over the water, watching the barges. Or gaze up at the stars as they sailed overhead.

In winter it would sometimes get so cold that chunks of ice formed in the river and one February the Thames froze solid from bank to bank. The warmth of the sewage formed a small pool right by the outlet, but beyond it the only navigation on the water was by foot or skate.

That weekend there was a Frost Fair, with dozens of different rides and stalls, and it seemed the whole city was marching up and down and drinking beer and falling over, as if the Thames was just any other thoroughfare.

The bears sat and watched from the shadows, until it was time to take up their hoes and shovels and return to work. But on the Saturday afternoon a young child spotted some movement up the tunnel. He'd taken twenty steps and stopped at the ice's edge before his mother missed him. She turned and went scurrying after him.

'Did you see them?' the child asked his mother as she led him back towards the bright lights. 'Did you see the bears?'

———————

Three months later a dozen or so bears sat on that same ledge, looking out at the water. The river was still and quiet. Some of the bears were already dozing, when a barge slowly swung into view.

Something about the boat's progress caught the bears' attention. It lacked the decisive nature of most barges: their blunt determination. In comparison, this barge seemed positively aimless. The fact was that its captain, having worked like a dog for two days solid, and having been up and down the river twice already today, and having just picked up his last load of coal and being on his way back to Limehouse, must have relaxed a little – in fact, relaxed to such a degree that his chin now rested on his chest, his eyes were closed and the wheel was doing nothing but support his hands.

The bears watched as the barge advanced at a sideways angle, then came right at them. They'd seen plenty of barges over the years but none had ever come within twenty yards of them.

It's bound to turn, they thought. Bound to turn away at any moment. Until, one by one, those moments all ran out and the bears had to allow that the barge's collision with the gate was a possibility, then a probability, then imminent.

If the barge had been empty it might not have made such an impression, but those forty tons of coal ensured that, even after the initial impact, the barge kept on coming – kept on driving right up the tunnel.

The bars popped out of their footings, the gate went under and was dragged squealing for twenty feet or more. The barge continued – straight up the main drain, until its prow was right among the bears. It paused there for a couple of seconds, as if considering its new surroundings, then slowly withdrew; slipped back into the river and drifted, backwards, towards the opposite bank.

The captain was awake now, along with every bear in the sewers. Those dozing by the main gate had jumped up at the sound of the collision. But throughout the city's pipes and drains there was a moment when the bears froze and turned in the direction of the commotion. Then they were all heading towards it as fast as they could.

The bears had no way of knowing whether the river

they'd looked out at all their lives would support them or take them under. It seemed quite reasonable that they would be able to swim, but it was nothing more than an inkling. So having waded tentatively into the water they were mightily relieved to find that the river actually buoyed them up.

London continued to go about its business, oblivious. It was late, but hundreds of people still went up and down the Embankment and crossed the bridges of Southwark and Blackfriars. There appeared to be some fuss on the south bank of the river, but nobody spotted the great huddle of bears as it drifted within fifty yards of them.

The bears instinctively knew that too much movement would only draw unwanted attention. Besides, the tide was on the ebb and so, just as it supported them, it also drew them east, out of the city. And when the river widened the bears finally felt safe enough to do a little paddling of a more concerted kind.

They came ashore, wet and cold, on Two Tree Island, a few miles short of Southend-on-Sea, and sat on the beach wondering where on earth they were, what direction they should be going and where their next meal might come from.

On securing its release a creature which has long been imprisoned might suffer a moment or two's profound anxiety – might experience something which could be misconstrued as misgivings, or uncertainty. But it is nothing more than disorientation. And so it was at Two

Tree Island. The moment came and went. The bears got to their feet, brushed themselves down and headed north.

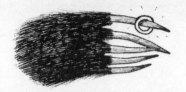

6

Civilian Bears

There have always been rumours of bears living among us. But at the very outset we should make a clear distinction between the subject of this chapter and those wild bears which occasionally stray into a town's outskirts, upsetting dustbin lids and dogs, not to mention dogs' owners, when their regular supply of food runs dry. Our only concern here is that bear which, one way or another, deliberately sets out to inveigle its way into society; to dress itself up in such a manner that it might live the same life of unmitigated tedium as the rest of us.

Such tales of deception often seem to originate in England's working-class communities. There are reports of bears carrying sides of beef on their shoulder around Smithfield Market, a bear employed as an assistant at a hardware shop in Rishton, Lancashire, and several bears said to have worked as miners in the pits of Durham and Nottinghamshire.

Two separate reports from the 1920s refer to a man of 'bear-like appearance' being employed in hotels in East Anglia – the first at a traditional establishment in Cromer, the other in the kitchen of a guesthouse in Southwold, although why a bear or bears should be drawn towards the catering trade is a mystery, beyond the obvious proximity to large quantities of food.

We should be somewhat sceptical of the woman in Dorset who, in the 1870s, claimed to have married a bear. As is the case in all these 'My husband/wife is a bear' stories, it is much more likely that her spouse simply had about him one or two ursine attributes, such as extra weight around the girth and nether region, a grumpy demeanour or general hairiness. It is also worth noting that the spouses of such 'bears' only seem inclined to make such allegations when the relationship has in some way broken down.

Reports of bear-publicans, bears in academia and bear-vagrants can all, to some degree or other, be dismissed as either fanciful or malicious, along with bear-postmen, prizefighters and pylon-painters. But over the years there have been, even at a conservative estimate, a good dozen or more well-documented instances worthy of consideration, and it is the intention of this chapter to collate all that is known regarding the best-known of these.

This individual went by the name of Henry Huxley. Little is known of his early years and general upbringing and, in truth, not a great deal more is known of the years that came afterwards. It is as if he simply landed, fully formed, in his deep-sea diving outfit on Brixham Harbour in the spring of 1931. There are no corroborated reports prior to that. There he stood, surveying the scene through the small circular window of his helmet whilst his associate, Jim Stooley, engaged a man in conversation not far away. Of the four or five occasions when one may say for certain that Henry Huxley plied his trade, Jim Stooley is always close at hand. One possible explanation is that Stooley had a better head for management and administration. Another is that he knew enough about deep-sea diving to appreciate the dangers and preferred to have someone else taking the risks, instead of him.

Whatever their relationship, it seemed to suit both parties. And as Henry Huxley checked his weights and fittings, Stooley and the harbour master went over the particulars of the job in hand. This was no everyday bit of underwater business. Several other private deep-sea diving contractors had arrived, assessed the situation and left without even bothering to give a quote. The problem, in its simplest form, was that some old nets from one of the trawlers had ended up in the harbour and any number of lines and anchors had proceeded to get involved. Unpicking a great granny knot of chain and net and cable was tricky enough, but became potentially fatal when one introduced the possibility of the pipe carrying a diver's air supply getting tangled in the mess.

So the advice from all previous parties had been to

leave well alone and for the local fishermen to berth their boats across the harbour. Whereas, even now Jim Stooley was shaking hands with the harbour master. Was going over to Henry and putting an arm around his shoulder and taking him off to a quiet part of the dock. According to those present, there was much gesticulation and gazing into the deep-sea diver's helmet as the breadth and depth of the problem was laid out, along with how they might realistically hope to sort it out.

Half an hour earlier, a manual air pump, apparently dating from the Middle Ages, had been unloaded and a couple of local lads had been drafted in and made fully cognisant of the two large wheels which cranked it into life.

'Just keep on winding,' Jim Stooley had told them. 'I'll tell you whether to pick it up or slow things down.'

And now Stooley was down in the harbour, hanging over the side of a rowing boat, not far from the ladder where Henry Huxley had last been seen. In his hands he held what he referred to as his 'viewing-box', which was basically just four sides of timber with a piece of glass fitted in the bottom and a brass handle on either side. Half the time he had his head inserted in it, trying to keep an eye on Henry's progress. The rest of the time he was looking over his shoulder, keeping an eye on the pump's various valves and dials.

If the arrows dropped too far to the left he would call out, 'Wind her right up now, boys. That's it. Give her some.'

If they threatened to swing too far to the right he
would call out, 'All right, lads. Now, lay off a bit. That's
it. You lay right back . . .'

In this manner the three of them kept the fresh air
flowing, whilst in the murk down below Henry Huxley
was busy unpicking. He had gone down the metal steps,
rung by rung, with nothing but a set of steel-cutters and
a bread knife tucked into his belt. When he re-emerged,
forty-five minutes later, he had a great chain over his

right shoulder. The rest trailed, dripping, into the harbour.

'Nah then,' said Jim Stooley and turned to the locals. 'There's your problem.'

Stories of Huxley's formidable strength are confirmed by the locals who watched as he stood on the harbour wall and dragged that chain out of the water, fist over fist. There was some debate as to what might be at the end of it, the majority betting that, judging by the speed it was emerging, there would be very little at all. But they were proved quite wrong when out of the harbour there emerged a sea-mine, quite rusty, but still spiked and lively-looking and swinging perilously close to the wall.

Within twenty seconds the spectators had vanished – most of them back home, to hide under the kitchen table and the rest up the hill, to get as far away as possible (whilst keeping the harbour in sight so that they might get a decent view of it if the whole lot went ka-boom). The only people left on the harbour were Huxley, Stooley and the harbour master, who would've run himself if all the blood in his body hadn't suddenly gone to his boots.

There was a brief exchange between Stooley and Huxley, with a fair amount of animation on Stooley's part. Then Stooley took a few steps back, to give him some room, Huxley got a good grip of the chain and slowly started spinning. Kept on spinning on the heel of one boot until the mine was flying at the end of its chain, about chest-high. Then, with one final, accelerating spin,

Henry leant back, raised his arms and let go, just like a hammer-thrower. And the mine flew out, over the harbour wall towards clear water, like a comet, with its chain for a tail – much to the delight of the locals up on the hill, who were just relieved that the diver had let go at the appropriate moment, or else the sea-mine would've been headed straight for them.

There was no explosion, which was a bit of a disappointment. All the same, the spectators burst into spontaneous applause. The harbour master shook the hand of Stooley and was on his way over to Huxley to do the same when there was an almighty thump, the sea erupted and, a few seconds later, a heavy shower of saltwater descended on the town.

The whole episode could so easily have resulted in utter carnage. On the other hand, it was dramatic enough to ensure that Stooley and Huxley's reputation went before them: a reputation, in short, for being prepared to take on the kind of job the rest of the deep-sea diving fraternity had too much common sense to go anywhere near.

Their next known job was up in Derbyshire. A local landowner had written and asked them to drop by whenever they were passing. He had some caves, he said, that he wanted to 'open up, for the benefit of the public', which was another way of saying he had hopes of creating for himself a nice little earner by charging people to have a look around. When Stooley and Huxley arrived and stepped out of their wagon the landowner was slightly surprised to see the diver already wearing his suit and helmet.

'Does 'e not get 'ot in there?' he said.

'He does,' Stooley was reported to have told him, 'but it doesn't bother him.' Then he turned the fellow around and asked him for more specifics regarding the caves.

The landowner led the way across the fields towards the pothole's entrance, all the while denigrating in the most vigorous terms the handful of divers who had already spurned the job.

'They're all too nervous about getting their pipes caught on the rocks,' he said, as if concern about having enough air to breathe was an unmanly sort of thing.

'There's the two caves up front,' he said, 'neither of which is anything special, and then just *wather*.' The word 'water', pronounced thus, gave it an extra splashi-ness. 'I wants to know what's on t'other side.'

Derbyshire, the landowner informed Stooley, was famous for its underground chasms and chambers. And he was quite determined that beyond the flooded cave, there should be chasms and chambers of the highest quality. When they reached the entrance to the cave Stooley happened to ask what he planned to do about the water-filled cave, if his hopes for those beyond were found to be justified.

'Well,' he announced, quite casually, 'I'd just blast an 'ole reet through it.'

Huxley was standing nearby and looked up, to see if the landowner was joking. It seemed he wasn't. In fact, the landowner was already describing the many gantries and catwalks he'd commission, for the many paying visitors he expected to file through. Stooley happened to glance over at Huxley. He was still staring at their client as if he was a complete lunatic.

Again, before the work commenced Stooley took Huxley aside and gave him a few private instructions. The landowner noted how Stooley raised a flattened hand and made a dipping motion, presumably to explain how he was going to have to drop down into the water, before coming up into the cave beyond. Then he fitted the pipes, tightened the bolts and led Huxley over towards the hole.

Stooley lit the phosphorous lamp and fastened a rope to the canvas belt around Huxley's waist. The previous evening they had tied their four longest ropes together, to cover all eventualities. Three sharp tugs from Huxley and Stooley would do his best to try and drag him out.

Stooley worked the pump's wheel himself and watched as the ground slowly swallowed his colleague. The entrance to the caves was nothing but a small slit in the field. Once inside, Huxley lifted his lamp and carefully made his way through the first cave, then into a second. The lower section was flooded with water, which looked as black as oil. Huxley carried on, into the cold water, and must've dropped twenty feet or more down a bank of shale before the ground levelled out again; the phosphorous lamp illuminated the rock's low ceiling and he began to climb the bank of shale on the other side.

The first cave Huxley came out into was wreathed in ferns and lilies. The next seemed to extend a quarter-mile to left and right, like an underground ballroom. The third chamber had a waterfall in it – a narrow jet of spring water that fanned out in a spray so fine that it fell as mist on the rocks a hundred feet below. The fourth was a maze of stalagmites.

Huxley advanced like an Edwardian astronaut. He went as far as his rope would allow. Then he sat on a rock and looked about him. He sat and looked about him for quite some time.

It just about goes without saying that bears and caves have a certain affinity. Perhaps this is why Huxley was so repulsed by the idea of someone blasting his way through all that rock and having a steady queue of people marching through such a magnificent place.

When he finally emerged a good half an hour later the landowner headed straight over towards him and was tapping on his little circular window before Stooley could insert himself between the two of them. Stooley insisted he remove the helmet a little way off, without interference – then got his spanner on the case.

The helmet was lifted off and the landowner watched as the two of them gesticulated wildly at one another. He wondered if some earlier accident had perhaps robbed the diver of his speech or hearing.

But when, a couple of minutes later, Stooley strode back over to the landowner he had a forlorn expression on his face.

'He reckons . . . as you say . . . that it's just water,' he said. 'Just water. Then solid rock.'

For the landowner it was a bitter pill to swallow. But that particular moment in time has extra significance in that it could be said to pinpoint the beginning of the end of Huxley and Stooley's relationship. Driving back to their digs that afternoon the air was thick with resentment. Stooley strongly suspected that there were indeed more caves down there, beyond the water – fancy chasms and chambers which they might have been gainfully employed blasting their way through to for months on end. Instead, those same months would be spent driving up and down the country, exhausted, chasing nothing but the occasional day's work. Stooley managed to keep a lid on it for the best part of twenty minutes before finally exploding.

'You used every last inch of that rope,' he said, without taking his eyes off the road for a second. 'Every damned inch of it.'

———————

Their next couple of jobs were nothing special: a few underwater repairs to the docks down at Harwich and some work on a stretch of the Leeds–Liverpool canal. Then they received a letter from Winchester Cathedral. Apparently, the crypt had flooded and a preliminary investigation had revealed that the foundations actually consisted of great slabs of beech, which were so thoroughly rotten that the whole building threatened to capsize, like some vast stone ship, into the fields of Hampshire.

Stooley and Huxley pitched up within twenty-four hours and it was Stooley's private opinion that there was enough work there to keep them going for a good couple of years – maybe longer, if they dragged their feet. But they were still formally assessing the situation on that first morning and Huxley was forty feet beneath the south transept on only his third descent when Stooley fatally took his eye off the ball.

He'd been staring out towards the water meadows — dreaming of making enough money to buy a house down here and maybe a little boat to go with it . . . and meeting some local girl and settling down . . . and spending his Sundays sitting on some sunny porch . . . and eating bread and cheese, laced with fresh watercress . . . and maybe taking his young wife out on his boat at midnight for a bit of a canoodle . . . when the tug on the rope yanked him out of his reverie.

He'd been rowing instead of pumping. When he looked over at the main dial the arrow lay flat against the pin. Stooley started pumping again — madly pumping — and had the levels back up in less than ten seconds, but he knew better than anyone the possible consequences of his error. As he pumped he wondered whether he might have killed Huxley. Or given him brain damage. But two minutes later, Huxley appeared, fairly brimming with life. Stooley unfastened the bolts, lifted the helmet and still had a hold of it when Huxley floored him with a right hook — or, as the observers noted, not so much a hook as a sweep of an outstretched arm, but with sufficient force to send Stooley and the helmet flying a good ten feet.

Clearly, a company's professional reputation only suffers when its principal operators are seen punching and wrestling with each other on consecrated ground, and within the hour they were on their way. The contract was eventually awarded to one William Walker. His work among the flooded foundations of Winchester Cathedral would make him something of a minor celebrity, which did nothing but add to the bitterness already gnawing away deep in Stooley's gut.

———•◦•———

Ethel Braithwaite was long on years, but short on inches. In her prime she barely cleared four foot eleven, but past the age of seventy, it seemed, every year did nothing but diminish her more.

'The old girl's shrinking,' announced Ned, her youngest grandson. 'If she keeps this up we'll be burying her in a Weetabix box.'

Within a month he was rueing such flippancy. And if her coffin wasn't quite as small as he'd predicted it wasn't much bigger, and might easily have been mistaken for that of a child. Henry Huxley carried it down the shore of the Maddingly Reservoir. He could have tucked it under one arm without too much trouble, but for dignity's sake Jim Stooley had shown him how to hold it out in front of him. As always, Huxley was kitted out in his diving suit, the only difference being the spade tucked down the back of his belt.

He walked with measured step into the first few feet of water. This was no time to be tripping or slipping about. The coffin may have been modest but it was a fair old weight, for, as well as Mrs Braithwaite, it contained a dozen bricks to give it some ballast and help it stay where it was put.

The vicar sat bobbing in the shallows, flanked by two of

94

the younger Braithwaites and their mother. In the boat next to him another pair sat solemnly cranking the pump, under Stooley's supervision. A third sat over the oars. The remaining mourners were divided between four other rowing boats.

They watched as the deep-sea diver carefully waded into the water. When he was up to his waist Huxley let the weight of the coffin take it under. He carried on as the last bubbles of air came up from it. And a minute later he and Ethel were out of sight, with just the air pipe trailing after them.

After a moment's grace, Jim Stooley pointed out across the reservoir. The rowers leaned forward, then pulled back on the oars. And as Huxley carried on, down into the darker, colder water, the six boats came slowly after and over him.

It had been Ethel's dying wish that she be buried alongside her husband – the kind of request which ordinarily would have not been too hard to accommodate. But it had been ten years since the Braithwaites, along with thirty other families, had been removed from their homes, given a small cheque for their troubles, then watched as their village was effectively drowned. They saw the streets where they had played as children rush with water and their homes slowly slip from view. And the church where they had been married and where their children had been christened slowly sank beneath the water, until only the spire stood proud of it. Then the weathervane. Then that too was gone.

Now here she was again, at her own passing. The first
few spots of rain fell among the mourners and half a
dozen umbrellas sprung into bloom. One of Ethel's
daughters held hers over the vicar. Jim Stooley had his
viewing-box in the water and when his head wasn't
buried in it, monitoring Huxley's rather stately progress,
he was glancing over at the pressure gauges. He had no

intention of risking another beating like the one he'd had in Winchester. The bloody lunatic had very nearly broken his neck. If he ever made another mistake of that sort of order, thought Stooley, he'd better go the whole hog and make sure he didn't come back up at all.

The vicar sat hunched over his damp little book. His words came out of him in a low drone, like an incantation. Down below, the drizzle made not the slightest difference. The place was locked in a perpetual gloom. Wherever Huxley looked the view was vague and unsteady, like a world unconvinced of its own existence. He'd been given the most rudimentary co-ordinates and now did his level best to carry the coffin in the right direction. But he had walked for a good quarter of a mile and the air pipe didn't have much play left in it and he was beginning to lose heart when his boots finally struck solid ground. He looked down and saw cobbles – mossy cobbles, with weed sprouting in between. And as he advanced a dry-stone wall took shape to his right and, beyond it, the silhouette of a row of cottages. The next minute he reached the high street. A minute later the church spire loomed up ahead.

One of the cemetery gates was open. The other had broken free of its top hinge and leaned back, at an awkward angle. Up above, Jim Stooley studied the scene through his viewing-box.

'He's there,' he said, his words bouncing around in his box. 'He's at the graveyard.' And the other boats slowly paddled over to that patch of water where Jim Stooley was looking in.

Now, underwater digging can be a tricky business. Having taken some time to locate Stanley Braithwaite's headstone, Huxley gently placed his wife beside him, pulled out his spade and set to work. But every shovelful he took up became a cloud of dirt, some of which chose to settle, but much of which seemed to stay more or less where it was, until Huxley all but disappeared from view.

It took him a while to devise a way of lifting the earth without causing too much disturbance, and a great deal of very careful digging to create a hole deep enough to take Ethel's modest box. Huxley raised his head and looked up at the reservoir's surface – could just about make out the bottom of six boats drifting there. He took hold of the rope and gave it a single, sharp tug. Stooley saw the rope twitch out of the corner of his eye. He nodded at the vicar.

'Right, off you go,' he said.

The vicar didn't much care to be spoken to in this manner. On such occasions, as indeed in life in general, he was accustomed to being the man in charge. But his irritation was outweighed by his anxiety about being out on the water. As a boy he'd very nearly drowned on a boating trip in Yorkshire and ever since had done his utmost to keep as far away from boats as possible. At this moment in time he wanted nothing more than to have the whole thing over and done with and to be sitting back at home with a cup of tea, in front of the fire.

'We are gathered here this morning,' he told the attending Braithewaites, 'to commit to the earth . . .' then faltered as he looked around at all the water. He shook his head and carried on. '. . . Ethel Braithwaite – friend, neighbour and much-loved family member . . .'

Down on the reservoir bed, Huxley waited for roughly a minute, then lifted the coffin and held it over the hole. He let the weight take hold and slowly guided it in, until Ethel was finally back at her husband's side.

He took up his spade and began easing the earth back over the coffin. When he was done he patted it down and stood there for a little while. He turned and looked about him, much as he'd turned and looked about him in that spectacular cave beneath the fields of Derbyshire.

Up above, the boats were carefully turning and preparing to head back to the shore.

'You go on,' Stooley told the others. 'We'll be along in a minute or two.'

Again, the vicar wasn't particularly happy at having some grubby contractor doing all the organising, and was even less happy at having to hang about out in the middle of the reservoir for some deep-sea diver to plod back to the shore. After a couple of minutes he plucked up the courage to ask how much longer they might be called upon to wait out in the drizzle, but Stooley's head was deep in his viewing-box.

'Very murky,' he said.

As he was saying this, the lads who cranked away at the air pump felt the pressure suddenly plummet and the two of them went flying forward with such violence they almost fell right out of the boat.

The needles on both gauges dropped to the left, as dead as doornails. And even as Stooley stared at them, horrified, the water between the boats began to boil. The occupants of both boats turned and watched the bubbles break the surface. Then Stooley swore and inserted his head back into his viewing-box.

When he next looked over at the others his face was ashen. 'We've done nothing wrong,' he said, suddenly fearing an even more brutal beating than the last one. 'You're all witnesses. We did everything right by the book.'

The boys had ceased their pumping and it wasn't long before the water merely simmered, then grew quite still, and the only thing disturbing it was the rain. Stooley hauled up the pipe until it writhed about his feet like a great eel. He lifted the ragged end and stared at it, aghast. Then dropped to his knees, put his head back in his viewing-box, but could see nothing – no movement down there at all.

They rowed in circles for at least five minutes with nothing to show for it, then another five on top of that, until the vicar convinced them that they should return to the shore, if only to get the other boats out to bolster the search party, but the moment they reached dry land he leapt out and disappeared up the lane.

A whole flotilla of boats rowed from one end of the reservoir to the other, each with a fellow hanging over the side, to no avail. Stooley kept imagining Huxley emerging from the water like some monster, and each time he did so it got his heart a-thumping and made him feel very sick indeed.

In fact, years later he would be sleeping quite soundly when that dreaded deep-sea diver would come crashing into his dreams and Stooley would jolt awake in a cold sweat and, sometimes, screaming. Then he would have to get up and splash his face with cold water, just to calm himself down.

Stooley would always point out to anybody who'd listen how he had done all that could have been reasonably expected to recover his partner. But the world of deep-sea diving is tight-knit and riddled with superstition, and he never did manage to find anyone to take Huxley's place. He ended his days working the trawlers off the west coast of Scotland, which is about as hard a life as you can get.

Huxley could have abandoned Stooley on any number of occasions but contrived to do so in such a way as to inflict maximum misery. Bears are renowned for their incredible strength, but less well-known for their impressive lung capacity. A bear that puts its mind to it can hold its breath for several minutes, which in Huxley's case was long enough to split the pipe with his shovel and set about removing his diving suit.

The bear clawed away at the stiffened canvas and, just like Harry Houdini, wriggled his way out. And still had enough breath to swim the forty or fifty yards over to the church. We shall never know whether it was just good fortune or forward thinking when, having ripped away some of the spire's rotten roof tiles, Huxley located the old church bell, rusty now, but still containing a large pocket of air. It was stale air – ten-year-old air – but perfectly breathable and capable of sustaining Huxley until most of the fuss up above quietened down. Then it was another great lungful of air and a swim up to the surface, then over to the shore.

———•·•———

Jim Stooley went to his grave, still dreaming of blasting holes towards beautiful caverns and of idle hours sitting in the cathedral grounds in Winchester. The last time Huxley – or a bear-like figure – was spotted, he was headed east, through the gloaming, in the general direction of Derbyshire.

7

Bears by Night

In their turn, each tribe of exiled bear headed north, towards the colder counties. Hiked up into the hills and peaks, then went to ground. Made their way down, down into the darkness and settled, in England's forgotten caves and caverns. Growing still, until sleep came lapping at their ankles. Then deeper sleep came rolling in.

They slipped into the deepest, darkest hibernation, where circulation slows to a near-stasis and, finally, life itself hangs by a thread. Thus suspended, the bears abided, among the solid rock and the cold, cold stone. And the days began to spin, until they'd spun themselves into stillness. And the stillness fixed upon everything.

Up above, history slowly unfolded. The bears were oblivious – were cradled in the void. But, one winter's day, an age-old voice came struggling through the rock towards them.

Bears of England . . . came through the rock to them.

Some ancient winch flinched. Some rusty cable tightened. Tightened and began to turn. And the bears were slowly drawn back up the well towards their waking. The years . . . decades . . . centuries fell away. Until enough weary blood pushed and shunted round their aching bodies for them to blink an eye . . . swallow . . . raise their heads. And the bears slowly brought themselves upright. Began to make their way towards the light.

At the cave entrance the bears sat and looked out at the landscape. Nothing but snow all the way to the blinded horizon – filling the valleys, smothering the woods. The bears sat and stared, and let the light restore them, so that, after all those years of being fixed in darkness, they now found themselves fixed by light instead.

For that whole first day the bears just sat and waited, until the winter sun eventually fell behind the hills. Then they heaved themselves up and slowly set out across the pristine fields – no more than twenty bears in total, leaving nothing but twenty sets of prints in their wake.

The snow had fallen for four days solid, then drifted, obliterating all the walls and fences, erasing the roads. So that every home became its own tidy prison, and whole families gathered round the fire, and fretted about how much food they had in their larder, how many candles, how much fuel.

As the night pressed on and the darkness deepened the

bears picked up momentum. They headed out towards the east. Spent the whole night quietly marching, until the sky began to lighten. Then they rested, high on a moor, in the ruins of an abandoned cottage – bowed their heads, out of the freezing winds, until the light failed. Then raised themselves up and headed east again.

The next night their number more than doubled when they were joined by other bears, close to the cave where they'd spent their own endless hours of hibernation. And within three days every other last faction had been located, and quietly incorporated. Then that great battalion of bears swept around the valley and turned towards the south.

They followed the old ways – the old tracks and pathways. They let the mighty stars guide them home. And that age-old voice kept reaching out to them. Kept occurring to them.

Come, the Great Bear told them, *Bears of England, come.*

On the fourth night they came across a tiny church on its own small hillside, apparently empty. So the bears crept in and spent the daylight hours sheltering there. Perhaps a church has cave-like qualities. Perhaps it is something to do with stone. Whatever the reason, at the end of the next night's march they managed to track down another remote church and spent the day there, resting among the pews.

But at the third church, around midday, the bears were woken by a persistent thumping. The sound came juddering through the walls and floor. The bears lifted their heads and looked about them as, outside, old Mrs Earnshaw kicked her boots against the porch wall to clear the snow from them. It had been almost a week since her last visit and, barring illness and bad weather, she liked to call in at the church every couple of days.

The bears heard the clatter of the latch as it lifted – heard the creak of the hinges on the old oak door. Then Mrs Earnshaw entered, closed the door behind her, shuffled in, past the font and the shelves of hymn books, and slowly headed down the central aisle. Quite by chance, the pew she chose to sit at was completely empty. A couple of bears lay under the pew behind her and three more were laid out under the pew in front. Mrs E. leaned forward, rested her elbows on her knees and lowered her forehead onto her folded fingers. For nearly a minute she barely moved an inch. The occasional whispered word spilled from her lips, but her eyes remained tight-shut the whole time, as if to contain her prayers and help them on their way.

The bears stayed low. One or two stole a glance at the intruder. Others looked over towards the door, to see if any other ladies might be coming along behind. Then Mrs Earnshaw said 'Amen' out loud, sat back and had a look around her.

She sniffed the air. 'Musty,' she thought, and made a mental note to open up the doors and get some fresh air through the place just as soon as things warmed up a bit. She looked up at the stained glass (the Lamb . . . the Apostles), the roof, the pulpit – all as familiar to her as the fittings and features of her own living room. Then she got to her feet and headed for the altar, before banking to the right, towards the harmonium.

Half a dozen bears had been sleeping in the choir's stalls. They were

awake now – stock-still, listening. Could smell the soap
Mrs Earnshaw had used to wash her hands and face that
morning, along with the bacon she'd had for breakfast
and the whiff of mothballs that clung to her coat. She
lifted the harmonium lid, made herself comfortable,
pulled out five or six stops and began pumping away at
the pedals with her feet.

Some people hike. Some people go cycling. Mrs
Earnshaw liked to play the harmonium. Her boots went
back and forth with formidable industry, producing all
manner of squeak and wheeze and creak, until, having
worked up sufficient steam, she set both hands down on

the keys and the opening chords of '*Stand up, stand up for Jesus . . .*' filled the church.

A palpable jolt shot through the bears in their various hiding places. They were filled with a powerful urge to break cover – to run . . . to roar. But they held fast. They gritted their teeth and kept their heads down, wondering only what strange assault they were being subjected to.

'*There's a wideness in God's mercy . . .*' was not so dramatic. '*A Pilgrim through this lonely world . . .*' had a sweeter melody. And by the time Mrs Earnshaw got around to '*In full and glad surrender . . .*' and '*All the past we leave behind . . .*' some of the bears were beginning to find the experience strangely soothing, especially when the old lady's left hand reached down towards the lower keys and the whole church seemed to resonate in a warm and kindly way.

Mrs Earnshaw was quite at home with each hymn's first two or three verses, but by the time she reached the fourth or fifth her conviction would sometimes falter, and her singing would give way to periods of humming, until she found her bearings again.

The only potentially awkward moment arose about thirty minutes into her recital. She was midway through the second chorus of '*The day is past and over . . .*' – admittedly, one of the quieter hymns in her repertoire – when she thought she heard something like a *sigh* behind her. A sigh, but not necessarily human. More like the groan of a large dog as it lies before the fire. She lifted her fingers and glanced over one shoulder. Then the other.

111

She turned and surveyed the entire church. Most peculiar, she thought. Then she shrugged, turned back, did a bit more pumping and returned to her unwitting bear-serenade.

Mrs Earnshaw finally went on her way an hour or so later, and as soon as the sky began to darken the bears went on theirs. In the days that followed the thaw continued, which encouraged more people to venture out. And, having resolved to avoid the churches the bears were now obliged to find ever more obscure places to hide away during the daytime and wait until later in the evenings before setting out.

———⋅—⋅———

Every bear understood the nature of their pilgrimage. They saw no need for communication; had no desire to draw attention to themselves. But three days short of their destination, at the end of a long night's walk, with the sky in the south-east already shifting from black to blue, the bears happened to pass within half a mile of a block of kennels, where a pack of hounds was already up and waiting for their first feed of the day.

Within moments, bears and dogs sensed each other's presence. The bears stopped, turned, then headed over to the west. But it was too late. The dogs had caught their scent and were jumping at the fence, wild with excitement. Their master, Mr Stevens, had never seen the dogs in such a state.

Who knows what ran through the fellow's mind that morning? Perhaps he thought there was a fox at large. Perhaps, having saddled his horse and with the meadows still covered with untouched snow, he was looking for an excuse for an early morning ride-out. Whatever his reasoning, it seems quite likely that the dogs' excitement somehow got the better of him. For, without a word to his wife, he opened both gates and let the dogs go.

He never had a hope of keeping up with them. They were away and over the first fence before he had a foot up into a stirrup. For the first few minutes he just about managed to keep them in his sights – a mass of hound, three fields ahead of him. Then four. After that, he was simply chasing their tracks and their delighted yelps as they receded. By now he was riding flat-out himself, but he could hear how they were still getting away from him. Until, at the very point when they were almost inaudible, there was a sudden frenzy of barking and roaring and squealing. He pulled his horse up and listened, quite terrified. The awful noise continued for another couple of moments. Then abruptly ceased.

Five minutes later, he found the dogs at the edge of a forest, all ripped and rent apart – not a single one with a breath left in it; their blood and guts cast, steaming, across the snow. And coming upon them, Stevens's first thought was that this must be the work of some devil – some night-time demon that had somehow strayed into the light.

The bears pressed on. And all the while the call grew stronger.

Bears of England, come, the voice declared.

They did their best to avoid the towns and villages. They kept to the woods and the deeper shadows – kept their noses to the wind. But they eventually reached a river which struggled with all the water that had come off the thawing hills and fields. And for a while the bears had no choice but to walk along beside it, until they saw the bridgetown up ahead.

Unknown to the bears, the village was completely divided – had effectively been cleaved in two. The river had risen by six feet and was still rising. And whilst the bridge across it had managed to stand for three long centuries, the local constabulary, in the form of PC Harkins, was concerned that if some tree, ripped from the bank five miles upriver, should come hurtling down the torrent and strike the bridge's footings, then that tree, together with the water's force and debris already piled against it, could quite conceivably bring the whole lot tumbling down.

So, the day before the bears arrived, the bridge had been closed, for public safety. Which meant that, not only did every van and lorry have to add another twenty miles to its journey, but any villager who happened to find themself on the wrong side of the water was now effectively homeless and obliged to fall back on the hospitality of friends.

For the first couple of hours people gathered at the

bridge, in festive spirit, and called out to each other across the river's roar. And one clever dick had announced through cupped hands that he was short of a loaf of bread. Since most of the shops were on the north side, another villager had duly gone up the road, bought a bloomer and, on his return, done a reasonable job of hurling it over to him. But, towards the end of its flight, less than six feet from the outstretched hands of its intended target, the wind got a hold of it and sent it sailing down into the threshing water. And the villagers on both sides leant over the wall and watched it bounce between the rocks and foam, before finally going under and failing to come back up again.

A little later, someone had the bright idea of flinging two ropes across the bridge and knotting them together, to form a single giant loop. Then they attached an old crate to it and filled it up, like a Red Cross parcel, with some of those items that the villagers were in need of on the other side. And in this way, they managed a couple of successful deliveries – under the watchful eye of PC Harkins who, despite his best efforts, could see no good reason to intervene.

But on the third trip, just after it passed the halfway mark and began its slow descent towards the south side, the wooden crate hit a ridge of ice and toppled over. And the bottles of milk and loaves were tipped out, along with a small stack of post.

Everyone immediately turned to look at Eric Whalley, the postman, who had been most reluctant to hand over the letters in the first place and had only done so under extreme duress. His face was red and getting redder. He looked as if he was about to burst into tears.

In fact, the letters were in no immediate danger – they were bound together with an elastic band and pinned to the ground beneath a two–pint milk bottle. Even so, they were now neither in his sack nor on the addressee's doormat, which, as far as Eric Whalley was concerned, amounted to some sort of postal limbo, which was a state quite capable of costing him his job.

At this point, PC Harkins finally stepped in, insisting that no one should either touch the rope or make any attempt to retrieve the crate. And not long after he put up a sign on his side of the river strictly forbidding access under any circumstances and called out to a couple of fellows on the other side to do the same.

Most people slipped away not long after, and by the time the sun had set the remaining villagers drifted home themselves. When, twenty minutes later, PC Harkins turned to go, Eric Whalley grabbed him by the elbow.

'Where're you off to?' Eric asked him.

'Where do you think?' PC Harkins replied.

'But you can't leave the bridge unmanned,' said Eric.

PC Harkins told him that indeed he could – that he was not about to spend the whole night getting frostbite on the off-chance that some halfwit tried to creep across it, since if they did then that would be entirely their lookout, and nothing to do with him.

He placed a reassuring hand on the postman's

116

shoulder, in a manner that was not altogether different to how he might arrest a man.

'Trust me, Eric,' he said. 'Those letters'll still be there in the morning.' His expression brightened. 'And if the water's dropped we'll maybe open up the bridge.'

But the postman wasn't reassured in the slightest. The only point at which he envisaged feeling any improvement was when those letters found their way back into his sack. He wouldn't sleep a wink that night, he knew it. And he told PC Harkins as much. But this didn't stop Harkins heading off. So Eric headed home himself, made a flask of tea, grabbed a couple of blankets and a chair from the kitchen, then returned to the bridge.

For the first couple of hours Eric just sat and looked out from his huddle of blankets – a vigil interrupted only by him getting up at regular intervals to stamp some blood back into his feet and check that the letters hadn't blown away. But soon after midnight he observed how his thoughts were starting to wander and how his breathing was starting to slow. Curiously, he found that the further he strayed from consciousness the warmer his body became, as if sleep

117

brought with it its own intoxicating heat. But his mind was so utterly fixed on that small clutch of envelopes that, even though he desperately craved sleep and seemed almost powerless in the face of it, he was incapable of fully surrendering to it, jerking awake at the last second, to find himself back among the blankets. Each time, he would look around, quite startled. Then, a minute later, slowly start to slip away again.

On at least half a dozen different occasions Eric watched as some fellow came creeping across the bridge towards him. Saw the stranger stop by the crate and reach down towards the envelopes. And each time Eric would jerk awake, heart racing, to find the bridge quite empty, and all the cold night air would suddenly come rushing back in again.

The same vision occurred and re-occurred with such frequency that he began to consider creeping out onto the bridge himself, despite PC Harkins's orders. Began to think that the risks – of the bridge collapsing and him drowning – might well be worth it, just so that he could retrieve the letters and go home and pull the sheets up around his ears.

He considered this option for so long and with such fervour that, in the end, he simply cast aside the blankets and went down on all fours and did indeed creep out onto the bridge and reached those letters – took them up, tucked them inside his jacket – only to jerk awake again.

Mercifully, not long after, he slipped into some sort of stupor – a strange and dreamless interim, in which he was aware only of his own formless soul floating out among the elements. Neither bliss nor fear. Just being. And he had a sense of movement all around him – a wave of animal warmth slowly washing by him on both sides, as if it might carry him away with it. And he was perfectly at peace until, from the very depths of himself he heard a voice inform him, quite matter-of-factly, that he was now at the brink of extinction and that if he didn't wake up immediately, his heart would give out, his blood grow cold and that would be the end of him.

He was still debating whether he had the strength to drag himself back to consciousness, aware of the excruciating pain that would be waiting for him there. And he had yet to make up his mind, one way or the other, when he thought he picked out, in the furthest possible distance, the chink of milk bottles. And suddenly his will was restored and he drove himself back to the bridge and the blankets, and forced his eyes to open up.

As he came to, he thought he saw some movement across the river. He tried to focus. Thought he caught sight of some figure as it retreated into the shadows. His heart was beating again now – ten to the dozen. And as he looked out over the bridge he happened to notice that the crate halfway across it was apparently upright – had somehow contrived to untopple itself.

The postman wondered if this wasn't some other elaborate dream or hallucination. But the terrible discomfort he felt as he got to his feet told him otherwise. He looked out into the night, but saw no movement. Then he bent

119

down and started pulling the rope in – very carefully, so as not to send the crate over again. And, long before he had it in his possession, he could see just how neatly the contents of the crate had been organised, with the letters tucked between the empty milk bottles and no sign at all of the loaves of bread.

As he lay in his bed that night he could come up with only two possible explanations, neither of which was likely to satisfy PC Harkins. Either some villager, riddled with guilt, had crept out and righted it. Or, in his stupor, Eric had crept out there and righted it himself. The disappearance of the bread and milk was a quite separate mystery. And to be fair, the possibility of bears being involved never entered his head.

8

The Great Bear

Who'd bury a boat? It was, the boys felt, a quite reasonable question – a question which, having formed in their heads, had proceeded to become lodged there almost as stubbornly as the boat was lodged in the ground. The fact that the mound where they'd discovered the boat was so high above sea level did nothing but add to their bewilderment.

Other people had their own ideas, but as far as the boys were concerned the only rational explanation was that at some point in distant history there had been a flood of such biblical proportions that the hilltops had been transformed into tiny islands, and the boat had been beached there – or conceivably even built there, like Noah's Ark.

Now, deep in the night and with the mist thickening up all around them, the boys sat on the mound with their arms wrapped round their knees to try and generate some precious heat. Another three or four hours, they reckoned, and there might be a little daylight and, surely, no self-respecting looter of buried boats would go about their thieving business once the sun was up.

One of the boys had a torch and, at the other's insistence, he turned it on to cast a bit of hope about the place. But the torch's meagre beam did nothing but give the mist more substance, so it was soon turned off again. Then the boys just sat in silence, thinking how cold and uncomfortable they were, each one secretly hoping that the other might suggest abandoning their post so that they could go back home to bed.

The mound on which they sat was a familiar landmark – so familiar, in fact, that when they'd climbed up onto it only a week or so earlier to look out over the Levels, the boys couldn't help but notice how something in its shape was slightly altered. A whole section of the ridge along the top appeared to have sunk a little, as if some minor collapse had occurred deep within it. And when they went

down on their hands and knees they saw how the surface was laced with hundreds of tiny fissures and crevices.

Within the hour the boys had located a pick in a neighbour's shed, had quietly removed it and were staggering back up the hill with it. That blasted pick was as heavy as an anchor – was such a weight that they had to carry it between them, taking turns at the business end.

Neither boy was entirely sure what they hoped to discover, but whatever it was they spent a good half-hour desperately hacking their way towards it and creating a hole almost two foot deep, turning up in the process a small heap of grit and chalk and gravel, before the pick had become so utterly unwieldy that they'd given up, in part through sheer exhaustion and in part through fear of serious injury.

The boys sat on the mound while they got their breath back, their shirts drenched with sweat. They stared out at the view before them, but as they talked one of them picked over the pile of earth, and was paying very little attention to it when he caught a glimpse of a tiny face staring up at him through all the soil and stones.

It was a strange, expressionless face. He picked it out and brushed the dirt off it. Just a smooth old stone, with a single scratch for a mouth and two blind eyes marked on it – features which looked as if they had been there for all eternity.

The boys spent quite a while wondering what to do with it. Simply looking at the thing gave them the willies. They considered keeping it secret. Considered putting it back in the ground, well out of the way. But the boys knew that even burying it was unlikely to stop them thinking about it. So they carried it back down the hill and showed it to their parents – a decision which they regretted within minutes of doing so.

Half an hour later the boys were climbing that hill for a third time, in the company of their fathers, who then did their best to outdo one another with their own shovels and spades. And in half an hour they'd dug a hole four times deeper than their sons' effort and struck something solid and quite sizeable.

From that point on things progressed fairly swiftly, with more and more adults steadily getting involved. Alec Heydon, a local librarian-cum-historian, heard about what he felt amounted to an act of desecration taking place on what was very likely an ancient barrow and went haring up there and promptly requisitioned the entire site. Then, the following day, with a little help from one or two of his colleagues from the local archaeological society, he made his own discovery.

'Ribs,' he had announced to the small clutch of people gathered round the base of the barrow. It was the same term he employed in his letter to the professor at Oxford University, who duly jumped in his car and headed down the A420, post-haste.

'Full marks,' the professor told Alec Heydon soon after his arrival. 'Ribs, without a doubt.' Then he designated the site an official dig and drove straight home to pick up enough clothes and pipe tobacco to sustain him for however long the excavation was likely to take.

And then the word went round the village that ribs had been uncovered in that odd little mound overlooking the Levels. At the butcher's the customers speculated as to what sort of ribs exactly they might be dealing with. Human ribs? Ribs off a mammoth, maybe?

'Not ribs, as in a *body*,' Alec Heydon had corrected them. 'Ribs, as in a *boat*.'

When the professor returned he brought with him his own team of duffel-coated assistants, with their own special scrapers and brushes and sieves. Then the locals were herded back behind a rope, which created a fair bit of resentment, not least among the boys – and was tempered only by the fact that their fathers and Alec Heydon were herded back behind it alongside them.

But the following day, with the first fall of snow, the whole enterprise had suddenly ground to a halt. The professor didn't seem unduly worried. He simply installed himself before the fire at The Coach and Horses, with a book and pipe and a glass of porter and patiently waited for the weather to change.

'I don't mean to be rude,' Geoffrey Baines, the barman, asked him, 'but aren't you afraid someone might come along and steal whatever's buried up there?'

The professor smiled and took another sip of his porter. 'The only way anyone's going to be stealing anything from up there,' he said, 'is if they happen to have their own gang of navvies. That ground's as hard as steel.'

And this utterance too quickly entered circulation, as if it had been handed down by some great oracle. The boys were briefly heartened by it. But once the snow had stopped and the thaw had started, their buried boat again seemed suddenly vulnerable. The boys convinced themselves that news of their ancient boat had spread well beyond the village and that somewhere out there someone was plotting to steal it away. And no sheet of tarpaulin, frozen stiff and held down by rocks, was going to contain it. So they had taken matters into their own hands and, late at night, crept out of their bedroom windows and hiked up the hill to keep an eye on the mound and the boat moored deep inside it.

The first night had been a bit of an adventure. And when the moon crept out between the clouds and cast its

126

icy light across the Levels it was as if a whole other world had been revealed to them – a strange and dangerous place which had almost nothing in common with its daylight equivalent. But on this second night they had sat and watched the mist come up around them. And after an hour or so had begun to feel quite cold and tired, and the novelty of being out in the night had suddenly worn quite thin. And what had, the previous night, seemed rather magical, now seemed downright dreadful and the boys began to sense that the mist had, hidden in it, all sorts of awful, unknowable things.

Neither boy had said a word for what felt like hours when one of them suddenly turned and squinted off into the mist. He was listening hard now, his eyes casting about for something concrete – something tangible. He slowly lifted a finger. The other boy looked over in the same direction, then shook his head. But the first boy continued listening, and the same raised finger shifted an inch or two to the right. And now they were both aware of it, whatever it was. Some sense of movement. Something moving in the mist.

The boys slowly got to their feet, still listening. And began to appreciate that whatever was out there was a great many in number – moving and breathing, and coming this way.

They crouched back down and, still facing forward, and with their eyes still searching, began to creep back off the mound. When they got to the bottom they turned and headed off into the fog, in what they sincerely hoped

was the opposite direction to whatever advanced towards them. They scrambled away, backs bent and hands picking over the ground before them. But they had no idea where they were heading and arrived, quite suddenly, at a sheer drop, and one of the boys had to grab the other to stop him going over. Then they crept along the ridge, in search of some other way off the hilltop. And as they came around they saw the figures in the mist. There must have been a hundred or more of them – huge figures – moving with great conviction. The boys froze. The procession continued before them. But the moment the boys thought that most of the figures had passed them they got to their feet and ran.

They could have gone straight home – could have crept back into their beds and no one would ever have known what they'd been up to. But without a word being exchanged between them they raced around to The Coach and Horses and started hammering away at the front door.

The moment their fists struck the door a peculiar thing happened. The boys started crying – great breathless gulps, quickly followed by floods of tears. As if it had taken that sound or that simple action to break the spell and release them. Then all their emotions suddenly came tumbling out.

Geoffrey Baines was fast asleep and it took him a couple of minutes to come around, lay his hands on his dressing gown and find his way downstairs, by which time half the street was hanging out of their windows to see what was going on. Baines was still barely awake when he opened the door and found the two boys in such a state on his doorstep. But as soon as one of them managed to blurt out 'Get the fella', Geoffrey knew precisely which fellow they were after and turned and headed straight up to his room.

The professor was led down to the bar in his pyjamas and then the boys finally felt able to say out loud exactly what they'd seen.

'It's the navvies,' said one, hitching a thumb over his shoulder.

'The navvies . . .' the other added, '. . . come for the boat.'

The mist was clearing now, the stars blinking back into existence. The bears had clawed most of the dirt off the top of the mound and were hacking away at the earth around the base.

The deeper they dug the darker the soil became, until the full curve of the boat was revealed – forty foot from bow to stern and eight foot across the gunnels.

Bears of England, the Great Bear told them, *make haste*.

Anyone who'd managed to sleep through the boys hammering at the door of The Coach and Horses was woken not long after by the sound of people charging up and down the street.

'Looters, up on the hill,' they shouted. And they called out for men and weapons, if they had them, and any sort of light or lantern, to guide their way.

It took several minutes for the villagers to get themselves organised and to stir up a little spirit. Then they all went charging up the hill. And all that running and scrambling seemed to generate an extra dose of courage, so that they began to imagine that whatever adversary might await them on the hilltop, they would be able to overwhelm it – for the village's honour and the owner-ship of their earthbound boat.

But when they finally cleared the ridge they found the landscape quite transformed – almost unrecognisable. The earth that had once made up the barrow was now flung out on all sides, as if a bomb had been quietly deto-nated, leaving nothing but an empty pit.

As the villagers stood, dumbstruck, the bears carefully made their way down the other side of the hill with that ancient boat raised up on their shoulders – an earthy boat carried through the night. Some bears led the way. Some hung back to see if anyone followed. They took their time, but as soon as they reached the marshes they headed straight to the nearest channel, gently lowered the boat into the icy water and crept in alongside it.

They tucked their shoulders under the hull and pushed off. And carried the boat out, through the dykes and ditches, until they reached the deeper water. Then on, through the Levels and beyond, into the estuary.

Memories of bear-pits and dogs and baying children slowly receded. The Englishmen who'd hunted them, then briefly idolised them slipped away – along with London's sewers and high-wire walking, and bread and beer in exchange for dead men's sins. And the bears kept on paddling, just as some of them had once paddled their way to freedom down the River Thames.

As they passed the headland the sun slowly rose behind them. And they continued paddling, out into open water now. Until England itself finally began to diminish – began to slip from view. One or two of the bears glanced over their shoulders. Had one last look at cold, cruel England. Then they turned away, and pushed on again.